AD LUMEN PRESS

American River College

LOIS ANN ABRAHAM

CIRCUS GIRL

& other stories

Ad Lumen Press | Sacramento | 2014

The following stories have been previous published, often in different forms:
"David Fell and Karen Rose" and "Mates" (*Burning the Little Candle*);
"Donna's Story" (under the title "Virginia's Story") (*Her Own Voice*); "Little
Comfort" (*Watershed*); "Therapy" (*Chico News & Review*);
"Wayne's Left Hand" (*Convergences*)

Cover image utilizes photographs by NASA (public domain),
David Lewis Hammarstrom, and Kevin Closson,
used by permission of the photographers.

For information address: Ad Lumen Press
American River College | 4700 College Oak Drive | Sacramento, CA 95841
www.adlumenpress.com
Part of the Los Rios Community College District

Library of Congress Cataloging-in-Publication Data

Abraham, Lois Ann.
  [Short stories. Selections]
  Circus girl & other stories / Lois Ann Abraham. — First U.S. edition.
      pages cm
  ISBN 978-0-9911895-2-6 (pbk.) — ISBN 978-0-9911895-3-3 (kindle)
  I. Title. II. Title: Circus girl and other stories.
  PS3601.B688C58 2014
  813'.6--dc23

                           2014000531

First U.S. Edition 2014

Table of Contents

To T.O.

Circus Girl
& Other Stories

Circus Girl

Jill was the only girl who had ever run away from the circus, the only one she had ever heard of anyway. Many a seventeen-year-old towner had fallen for one of the roustabouts for his gypsy good looks and strong arms, or for a performer, whose job after all was to take the breath away. A girl like that would make a tour or two as a follower, a possum belly queen as the older people might say, part of the scene but never part of the family. Then she would drop off the train somewhere, maybe a better place than she had come from, maybe worse, probably pretty much the same. But Jill had taken the other route.

She had always assumed that she would be on the show for her whole life; both of her parents were zanies, and she knew the props and the moves like knowing how to breathe. But in her heart, she didn't think they were all that funny or interesting. Instead, the uncostumed, bare-faced audience fascinated her, what their lives must be like, the simplicity she saw in their expressions as they turned simultaneously at the ringmaster's command or a blast of fanfare and looked where their attention was directed, the innocence of what their homes must be, compared to the animal stink and drama and buzzing energy of life on the road, where the show went on and she was never alone.

When her lack of interest in the clown act was too obvious to overlook, first her concerned parents and then the gaffer had tried to talk some sense into her. As a kind of corrective measure, she had been sent out with the butcher crew during the come-in to sell programs, peanuts, and cotton candy from Oliver Mack's cotton candy stand. With her wares on a tray in front of her, she would pass through the crowd as they pushed towards the big top, pitching whenever she remembered to, trying to see what made these people so different. Then on the last night, the home sweet home performance of the tour, she spotted Reuben, blond, crew-cut, freckled, a perfect town boy.

He didn't even glance at her, but she liked his scrubbed good looks, so she followed him in and saw him sit down in the stringers to watch the clowns and wait for the main events. As she circled the tent, she kept an eye on him. She saw that he was alone, and the way he scooted over to make room for a couple with a little boy, not intruding but making himself available for conversation, told her he was lonely. Once the show actually came on, she gave up her half-hearted attempt

4

to sell and watched him stare with wide-eyed wonder at the exotic animals, the bareback riders, the aerialists and acrobats, glancing over once in a while to enjoy how the little boy was reacting. When the final act was finished and the ringmaster was declaring the evening a wild success in an accent fabricated to simulate a bigger, grander version of town talk, he stood up and headed for the exit, still alone, hanging back to let some older ladies stay together as they made their slow way out. She drifted behind him as far as the arch where the crowd had thinned out, and then he turned and faced her.

"How come you're following me?" he asked. His eyes were narrowed into a suspicious squint, and she realized he thought she was going to pick his pocket or trip him up somehow. She couldn't think of what to say, so she offered him a pink pillow of cotton candy on a cardboard stick. He shook his head no thanks.

"It's free," she said. "I'm giving it to you."

Reuben took the offering and pulled off a sticky wad. He put it in his mouth, and she wanted more than anything to follow it, to be sweet in that intimate space. He offered her a piece, and instead of reaching for it, she opened her mouth and let him place it on her tongue, where it melted and spread and disappeared.

"That over there," he said, " is my red truck. If you want, come with me and we can go for a little ride. I'll bring you back whenever you say."

She set down her tray of circus goods in the mud at the edge of the lot and followed him, not once looking back. The circus left town without her.

It might have been that night, or maybe the next one that she got pregnant. When they found out, Reuben changed in ways Jill hadn't anticipated and didn't understand. He no longer joked with her or played at tickling in the mornings to pull her into lovemaking. He insisted that they marry as soon as possible, so there couldn't be any gossip to cloud this child's sunny future. His folks, Nancy and Bob, were too sick to come down from Stockton, though they lent Reuben the down-payment on a little rundown house, and her parents, Glorianna and Willie, were already at ease in Florida, planning the next season's act. Jill and Reuben were both eighteen, barely, so they just got married at the county clerk's office with his cousin and a buddy from work as witnesses. Reuben picked up another job, just part-time on Saturdays, 10 to closing at the hardware store, and worked like a demon at his regular 8-5 at the lumberyard, picking up any overtime he could get. The baby was going to cost.

Jill tried to find a job herself to help out and pay for the impending hospital bill, but her big belly and her lack of the kind of experience wary owners of local businesses had any use for made it impossible.

"You don't have to work," Reuben told her. "I'll take care of it. You just stay at home and get ready for the baby."

She checked out all the library books on being a parent she could find and read them to Reuben over his dinner, or when he fell into bed, exhausted. He tried to listen, but her voice was so soft and pleasant that his eyes glazed over and then closed. She watched him sleep, his head so deeply sunk into the pillow, face painted with a film of fatigue, the tiny lines around his eyes making him look not older, but like a desperate boy driven by a man's fate. Even though he fell asleep, he encouraged her to keep reading, afraid that even if he did his part, she wouldn't know how to take care of the baby.

"Let's face it," he told her, "Glorianna may be an interesting person and all that, but she wasn't much of a mother. I mean, she was just a clown, after all. I don't mean any disrespect. She probably didn't know any better." He pictured a big-haired, painted-faced clown handing off the crying baby that had been Jill to another horn-playing, daffy, red-nosed fool to comfort, who would pass her on to a bearded woman wrapped in snakes. His imagination was not that far from the truth. He thought sometimes from the look on Jill's face that she might have calliope music running through her mind. It made him nervous, now that the baby was coming. He still thought of her as an exotic, a mermaid he had brought home from the sea and now had to cope with. She might not know how to raise a child on dry land in the real world.

Towards the end of the pregnancy, Jill's legs became numb and swollen and her blood pressure went up too high according to the doctor at the free clinic. During the weeks that followed, she lay in bed while Reuben took over the housework in addition to everything else he had tackled. She was amused at the way he went about it, buying different, presumably superior, bathroom cleanser like his mom had always used and a pair of enormous yellow rubber gloves he wore to wash dishes and left, neatly pinned together with a clothespin, hung over the little rack with the dishtowels.

When Stephen James arrived, he was a wonderful baby, handsome and sturdy; he was a difficult baby, cranky and wakeful. Even though he was helpless, Jill had the feeling he knew this was only a temporary state of affairs. Things would be different as soon as he figured out what was going on. He slept much less than she had thought he would, and she was awake many nights with his interminable ear infections and bouts of bronchitis, trying to keep him still to give Reuben his sleep. The quiet nights of holding him in her arms, watching him suck on her brown nipple and grow quiet himself under the influence of the warm milk, gave her the strength to continue even as it wrapped her in a blanket of fatigue. She felt like a metallic substance was running sluggishly in her veins, heavy and alienating.

Reuben was proud of his little son. He watched Jill anxiously when he was home to be sure she was handling the baby right, but he had to go to work every morning, leaving her to fumble through the day, trying to sleep whenever Stevie slept. He worried that her daze was depression, like in the books, and worried most of all that she would do something dangerous and hurt the baby, accidentally, subconsciously, on purpose.

"Why do you let him cry?" he asked. "Why don't you go get him?"

"He just needs to cry, I guess. If I comfort him and then put him down, he just cries again. I can't find any way to get him to sleep without crying. So I just let him cry. I can't stop him, you know. He just cries sometimes."

Reuben was concerned and searched through the pile of past due childcare books that were always out, usually left open to the last page consulted, where they had looked up diaper rash, colic, or teething. Most of the authors were clear that babies should not be left to cry. Then he found where Dr. Spock said that some babies cry to unwind, and to let them. He didn't tell Jill

9

what he had found, and he continued to worry anyway. The sound of crying was a trial to him, especially when Stevie's voice cracked with what sounded to Reuben like inexpressible, impotent, primal rage.

Just as Stevie's first teeth began to emerge from the rosy gums, he became ill once again, this time with diarrhea that was far worse than the side effect of teething listed in the books. His slimy diapers needed changing several times an hour, and he nursed listlessly or not at all.

Jill was up almost all night with him, holding him as he wailed or slept briefly, and woke to fuss again. In the morning, she was roused by the sound of toast popping up as Reuben fixed himself breakfast. The baby woke up at the same time, and she started to change his diaper, then realized it was dry. She packed him into his little plastic baby seat and went into the kitchen to consult with Reuben.

"Reuben, he seems really sick. He nursed a little in the night, but I think we need to call the doctor."

Stevie, set in his baby seat on the kitchen counter, was grim and unusually silent. As Reuben went to call, she leaned her tired body against the softly vibrating refrigerator, wanting to embrace it with her arms and rest her head on its top, but it was too high to reach. She could hear Reuben's voice, vital and warm, in the other room as he talked to the clinic.

When he came back, he seemed energized and full of adrenalin, authorized, ready to meet the challenge.

"We have to get some liquid into him, or he'll have to go to the hospital. He's dehydrating, and if he goes twenty-four hours without drinking anything, we need to check him in. They said give him flat 7-up or chipped ice if he doesn't want to drink."

"We don't have any," she said.

"I'll go get some. You finish packing my lunch for me, and I'll go get some. Okay?"

"Lunch?"

"Jesus Christ! Just wait here and I'll be back in a minute." He left shaking his head, rattling the keys in his pocket, moving so quickly that it took her a moment to realize he was gone, to regain her balance. Stevie was fussing and wriggling in his seat. She tried to get him to take water out of a spoon, but he turned his head away and glared at her. Reuben's open lunch box caught her attention, and she began mechanically to pack it with an apple out of the refrigerator and a peanut butter sandwich while Stevie cried.

When Reuben returned bringing the necessary supplies, he set them on the counter next to Stevie with the air of a man getting ready to change a tire. He emptied the ginger ale into a jar and shook it briskly to get the bubbles out.

"You hold him, and I'll get it down him," he ordered.

11

"Hold him?" She was unsure and felt unable to keep up. "I hold him?"

"Just hold his head," he said, dipping some of the liquid into a spoon. She held Stevie's smooth little face between her hands, so that when he turned his face to avoid the spoon, her hands turned with him.

"Hold him still!"

She took a firmer grip and held his face still, as Reuben tried to pry his tightly buttoned mouth open. Stevie opened his mouth to protest, and Reuben slipped the spoon in.

"There!" he said, but the baby had inhaled most of the liquid and began to choke convulsively, his face red and eyes panicked. She took him out of the infant seat, and held him with his face down, patting him on the back. When he stopped coughing, he cried in earnest, and the fear and anger in his voice set Reuben off.

"Hold him!" he said again. He seemed angry, backing up and balancing back and forth on his feet like a boxer. When she had set the frantic baby down again in the infant seat, Reuben stepped forward and seized a wooden spoon, putting it sideways in the wailing mouth to hold it open.

"Hold him still!" he yelled, and his eyes were so dangerous and unfamiliar that she obeyed him instinctively. She held the screaming baby against the seat while Reuben poured the ginger ale down

12

his throat, setting off another bout of choking which culminated in gagging and vomiting the little bit of milk he had taken during the night. She saw a small trickle of blood where the spoon had broken open his perfect mouth.

"This can't be right!" she pleaded, picking up their hysterical baby and holding him close. She wanted to put her hand over his mouth to silence the noise that was making her ears hum.

"Are you going to let him die because you're too weak to hold him down? You have to do it. Do it. Hold him again. Just hold him down."

"I can't," she yelled over the baby's goblin shriek. "He's bleeding. This can't be right."

"You don't get it," Reuben explained loudly. "If he doesn't drink, he'll die. Don't you understand that?"

"No, what they said is if he doesn't drink for twenty-four hours, he'll go to the hospital. Isn't that what they said? Not that he'll die."

"Do you want him to go to the hospital? Do you really think that's going to be good for him? Do you have any idea what that's going to cost?"

She couldn't think well enough to reason and be careful at the same time. "It's better than having your dad pry you open with a spoon," she said.

She thought for a moment that Reuben was going to hit her, but he hit the wall instead, cracking the plaster next to her head. She was suddenly aware that she didn't know what to do, not just about the baby, but about Reuben, about being here in this hard little house with this yelling man. She didn't even know how to continue to do the wrong thing. The two people she was closest to were both shrieking at her, both red-faced and upset; the baby's face was caked with a mixture of vomit, snot, and tears and her husband's spit was hitting her face as he yelled. She was still except for her hand, which continued to stroke Stevie's back rhythmically.

"Give it some time," she said. "They said twenty-four hours. Please, Reuben, I don't know what to do, but if he doesn't get better by noon, I'll call you. You're going to be late for work. It'll be okay, really."

She tried to get closer to Reuben, to give him the comfort of her warm body for a moment, to calm him, but he shoved her roughly away.

"How can you ask me to let him die?" he said. "He's my son."

"But it's not like that. It'll be okay," she said. "It really will. He's starting to calm down already. Maybe he'll get hungry."

"You say it'll be okay but you don't know anything about it. You don't know anything about what's real."

"Let's give it till noon. Call me at noon and I'll do whatever you say. I can't hold him down, but I'll take him to the hospital or whatever you say. Just let him calm down. Give me till noon."

"Goddamn you," he said, although he didn't usually cuss, and turned on his heel, slamming his way out of the house.

Jill set Stevie back in the infant seat where he began to wind down, and she sat on the kitchen stool and studied him. After a while, he quieted and returned her gaze. The house seemed especially still in the aftermath of the shouting, like when a show ended and left the performers cold and sore and tired.

"Okay, Steve-o," she said. "What the hell do we do now?" Stevie didn't answer. His round blue eyes were still wet with tears, and the look on his face was baleful and severe. The cut on his mouth had stopped bleeding and had already begun to heal. He began to cry again.

"I don't suppose you'd care for a drink?" she asked, imagining a large bottle of whisky and feeling her own tears rise for the first time. "I can't do this," she said. "This is something I can't do."

Her eyes wandered around the familiar kitchen, looking for inspiration among the pots and pans, the lunch box Reuben had forgotten to take, the dish soap on the windowsill in front of the polka-dot curtains, the yellow gloves hanging so neatly on the rack. On an impulse, she unpinned them and drew them over her shaking hands, hoping to feel something about

Reuben, to hold his hands, to be held. Then she held her hands open, fingers spread, on either side of her face, waggling her head, making a big fake smile. The baby fell silent at this. With her big yellow clown hands, she dipped up some ginger ale in a spoon and offered it to Stevie.

When he saw the enormous bright blob of color swooping towards his face, his jaw dropped and he swallowed the liquid automatically, intent on reading and making sense of this unfamiliar phenomenon, like nothing he had seen before. A dense yellow cloud, like a kite, like an oracle, smelling mysterious, intense, meaningful, it sailed toward him. Over and over, he watched the unprecedented yellow hand make the trip away and back, and he continued to swallow, entranced. She was quiet except for the tune she whispered just under her breath. Toot toot toodle-oodle toot toot toot. She let Stevie focus wholly on the astounding gloves, careful not to break the spell. When he had taken in a cup or so, he lost interest, so she wiped his face with a warm, wet cloth and kissed his firm cheeks.

She picked him up and lay down with him on the couch, where he began rooting at her front. She opened her nightgown and gave him her breast, and as he nursed, she let herself relax and fall asleep. The last sound she was aware of was the very faint hiss of Stevie's pee hitting the dry diaper. They both slept, and when Reuben came home for his lunch at noon, apprehensive and determined, he found them there and knew that it was all right, and felt obscurely that it was all wrong.

Dancing in Kansas

It's hard to understand how anything beautiful could flourish in Flatwater, Kansas. I was only seven and a half, but I knew ugly when I saw it and I hated Flatwater right away. The houses were sparsely scattered, the broken sidewalks empty of people, and as we drove down the two blocks of the only main street, looking for our new house, the horizon beyond town was an uncompromising, unbroken slash of brown dirt against the pale sky. A single tree, not much taller than me, stood in our grassless front yard. When we got out of the car, the air was dry and harsh and smelled like the inside of a box.

Flatwater was tiny, and the second-grade classroom I was thrust into had only nine children besides me. I don't know why it should have been true given the scarcity of children to play with, but the class structure at Flatwater Unified School was inflexible. Second-graders played exclusively with other second-graders of the same gender. Town kids stuck together, and farm kids, silent and abashed, with names like Gloria,

19

Deenie or Jolene, Lance, Elmer or Milton, were taken away in the stinky yellow bus as soon as school was out. So I was stuck with just three little town girls as possible playmates.

Because I had no sisters or brothers, I had learned early to entertain myself, setting up my dolls in fancy dress for elaborate banquets or devising ways to involve them in catastrophic accidents, using a red pen to draw bloody injuries on their plastic bodies so I could play nurse, bandaging them in strips of rags and dosing them with sips of water or imaginary pills. I used my markers to draw daisies and hearts and dog faces on the pages of my Big Chief tablet that was supposed to be for penmanship, and sometimes read books about magic and animals and brave little girls late into the night under the covers, long after my mother had kissed me and sent me to bed. So I had lots of ways to pass the time, but like all children, I needed someone to play with.

Jackie Rush and Martha Whitman were two of the town girls in my classroom, so I sought them out on the playground, but with little success. Jackie and Martha were next-door neighbors and claimed to be second cousins without being able to explain exactly what that meant. They were already best friends, had always been best friends, and intended to remain best friends forever. At first I was pleased when they allowed me to replace Jackie's little sister on one end of the jump rope, turning so that the two of them could take turns doing Red Hot Peppers, but I soon found that I was only there to serve, and the game didn't include a turn for me. They guarded each other like sheepdogs from my occasional attempts to enter into their pretend play and refused when I invited them to my house. Yet either of them would abandon the other without question, without looking back, and evidently without recrimination when summoned by the queen of the second grade, Charisse Powell.

Charisse was simply the most beautiful girl I had ever seen. Her beauty had nothing to do with the simpering smiles and dimpled cheeks of girlhood, which may charm adults but generally leave other children contemptuous or indifferent. Her face was a long oval with skin so pale and uniform that she seemed as though she would chip rather than bleed in the unlikely event that she were broken. Her hair was shiny, delicate, flossy blonde and curled the same way every day, around the sides and back, with one shapely little poof of curls poised delightfully over her brow. Her eyes were deep blue, rayed like those of a bride doll, and set at a slight downward angle, widely spaced and somewhat bored. Her mouth was generous and rose-colored, her teeth perfect, straight and white.

Her arms and legs were formed of the same

unblemished white flesh as her face, and I was horrified to notice as if for the first time the bruises, freckles, scabs and rough hairs on my own scrubby limbs. There was nothing of the imp or baby doll about her. She was tall, bossy, and infinitely sophisticated. She was regal, charismatic, and merciless. She ruled the second grade, and she knew it.

I wasn't in love with Charisse. I was obsessed and fascinated—possessed by an overwhelming, sickening envy that made my existence a weary and loathsome burden. To say that she was the prettiest girl in the second grade would be like describing the Grand Canyon as deepish. I was stunned, stupefied, and obliterated by her pastel perfection. She dominated my imagination entirely for most of the three years we lived in Flatwater with her commanding ways.

"That Charisse really has you buffaloed, doesn't she?" my brisk and kindly mother once remarked, shaking her head, inviting me to share her amusement. Buffaloed was a stupid, clumsy term for the intricately painful state I was in. Even given my mother's apparent inability to understand my pitiable situation, it was an enormous relief to be home instead of at school. Home was a cool, dark shelter for me after having been dazzled, dazed, and poisoned by Charisse's radioactive presence all day at school, where there was no escape.

"You're just as good as she is. Why don't you just

refuse to be intimidated?" My poor mother had no idea. She imagined that the difficulty was social, when in fact it was primal, organic, theological. I could as easily have stood in a fiery furnace, faithless as I was, and refused to burn.

It was impossible to compete with Charisse. On the first day of second grade, I took one look at her black and white saddle oxfords, the definition sharp and jaunty, and my brown and white ones seemed muddled, coarse, and second-rate. When my mother took me to buy school shoes the next August, I confidently chose black and white. On the first day of third grade, Charisse had brown and white, and the soft glossy chocolate color glowed against the vanilla background, making my black and whites strident and trashy.

The August before fourth grade, faced with the same inevitably wrong decision, I burst into tears in the shoe store, unnerving the salesman and embarrassing my mother and myself. I refused hysterically to say which shoes I wanted, held in the grip of predestined failure. I was way out of my league and I knew it. I was playing rock/scissors/paper with Aphrodite herself. My mortified mother chose black and white for me and hustled me out to the car. The pink shoe box sat between us on the car seat. I had no hope.

On the first day of school, I crammed my feet into

my new shoes and dragged myself lumpishly to school, hoping that Charisse wouldn't be there, knowing that she was inexorable. She stood in the middle of the sidewalk that led up to the school steps, incandescent and challenging. On her dainty feet were soft black suede loafers, velvety as a fawn's nose, the white stitching distinct and elegant against the rich, deep leather. Her face was no smugger than the last time I had seen her. Her victory was casual and inevitable, like gravity or time, and my defeat was all the blacker and more bitter.

Of course Charisse took ballet lessons. Her mother drove her into Liberal, fifteen miles away, every Thursday after school. She carried her pink leotard and pink satin slippers to school and then climbed into her mother's car with the ballet bag slung elegantly over her shoulder. My mother informed me at supper one evening that Mrs. Powell had offered to take me along if I wanted to take ballet lessons with Charisse. She had declined the offer without asking me. I was astonished and crushed.

"It's not really ballet, you know," she explained comfortably. "It's just fancy costumes and showing off."

After dinner I sat out on our bare, gritty porch and watched the sun go down behind our tree. I lost myself in dreamy fantasies of satin, tender velvet, sequins, soft feathers. I envisioned showing off, but with such flair and style that it was elevated to a fine art. I swirled and posed and grieved inwardly until the sun had set entirely and it was time for bed.

The Christmas play that last year was the usual mishmash of dolls and elves and Santa, pared down as usual to four large parts for girls and expanded to accommodate, but by no means spotlight, the six inarticulate boys. The Sugar Plum Fairy was a part that called for dancing, and naturally it belonged to Charisse. I begged to have the script amended to call for two Sugar Plum Fairies, craving the glory of being paired with Charisse like Snow White and Rose Red. My teacher assigned me the role of Mrs. Santa Claus with a firmness that left no room for debate.

Charisse rehearsed constantly, on-stage and off, until it drove me wild. She practiced on the small stage in the auditorium every lunch hour and after school, while I watched from the front row, livid with mingled admiration, resentment, and defeat. On Charisse's lovely face was the usual haughty but good-natured expression.

"You don't know ballet," she informed me, rising up onto her toes and twirling. "You don't know ballet and you can't dance." She turned languidly and sank into a deep curtsey.

"My mother," I said impressively, "my mother won a rhumba contest in New York City when she was seventeen."

Charisse drifted by, her arms raised, her face lifted in graceful rapture. As she passed, she gave me an ironic look and said, "You're lying, of course." And of course I was.

I watched Charisse practice ballet until I was so sick at heart I had to leave the auditorium. I should have just gone home, but I wandered feebly out into the late afternoon sun to the playground swings where I was too far gone for the elation of swinging. I could only sit on the hard seat and dig my feet into the dirt, making the swing gyrate in ugly patterns. I wanted to lie down in the heartless Flatwater dirt and be covered up and forgotten. I would not ordinarily have spoken to a mere third-grader like Deenie Poteet, but I was alone and ready for something to break. I was lonely and the torture of watching Charisse parade her perfections was driving me mad.

Did Deenie speak to me first? Most likely, since I was focused solely on my own misery. Her words must have been the ordinary ones used to transact the business of childhood: "Whatcha doin'?" "You wanna play?" "Can you come over to my house?"

Deenie was not only a lowly third grader; she was also one of the poor kids from the outlying farms who came to school with round purple sores on their bare arms, like scratched mosquito bites. I had been told in hushed tones that these were "dirt sores" and probably meant the kid had worms. Deenie looked a little dirty but healthy enough. She had olive skin and hair a shade lighter than her skin. Her shiny obsidian eyes were set flat in a heart-shaped face. Her thin mouth and smooth cheeks gave her an expression that was both sweet and inscrutable.

I went with her, knowing very well that her family was not "nice," that it was too late to do anything but go home, and that my mother would not have approved. In the savage mood I was in, I would have gone anywhere with anyone. I wasn't exactly hoping that something awful would happen, but I was wide open.

When we walked past Eddie's Oasis, the only bar in Flatwater, I was shocked that Deenie didn't cross the street and go down the other side like I always did. It seemed to me that when we passed in front of the dark, scary doorway, she deliberately took in a deep draft of sour, smoky, whiskey-laden air, and then she turned and smiled at me.

She lived outside of town down a road I didn't remember seeing before. When we came within sight of her place, she took me by the hand and led me around behind a small barn, and together we peered out towards the squat, rusty gray trailer. One window was blocked rather than curtained by a dingy, stained cloth. In the other was framed the head of a woman, her gray hair lank and greasy, gray skin loose, a permanent grimace marked in the lines of her face. Her teeth were bared in a long, yellow smile. Her face was like a dishrag used too long and left wadded up to sour. She seemed to be scrubbing potatoes.

"Is that your grandma?" I asked, expecting Deenie to get mad and deny it.

"No, that's my ma," she whispered, and she tugged me back behind the barn.

At the side of the barn was a primer-coated car, and the sound of our voices was momentarily drowned by the ragged revving of the motor. Blue smoke puffed out of the tailpipe. Inside the car was Deenie's older brother, Willard. I was ready to run. Willard was a big, stupid, slobbering boy of seventeen who had always seemed dangerous to me in his imbecile adolescence. His mouth hung open as he listened to the uneven roar of the car's engine.

Deenie's hold on my arm was surprisingly strong, and she dragged me backwards into the darkness of the barn. It was a velvet darkness, dusty, hay-smelling, but the wood underfoot was pleasant. As my eyes became accustomed to the dark, I saw that it was empty except for rags and empty cans, a stack of hay bales across one wall. The car engine stopped, and the tinny car radio began to play "Your Cheating Heart."

"What do you do here?" I asked in a whisper.

"Nothing," Deenie answered. "Dance."

"Oh," I said. "Dance." And I began to pirouette impressively, holding myself up for her admiration like a crystal figure turning in the sunlight. But when I looked, her eyes were almost closed and she was dancing herself, not like I was, not even like I could imagine. She was really dancing, and I stopped in mid-turn to watch.

She held her hands out to the front, clapping and watching them twist, then pulling her elbows back towards her body like the pistons on a freight train. Her hands rose up as if they would escape her and fly away home, and she coaxed them back with the rhythm of her shuffling feet and a tension in her torso that felt like fearful longing. With the sunlight behind her making me squint, she seemed to shimmer. She seemed surrounded by moving arms that carved the air into forms I could almost recognize but couldn't name before they had disappeared. I had never seen anything like it.

I began to do what she did, and she turned to me and smiled again. The patterns we made shifted before they were half-finished, and when the radio music stopped, we danced even more wildly, unleashed from the pedestrian rhythm. My shoulders shimmied my heart into a frenzy, and I felt a savage love for myself

29

which threatened to pull me into pieces. Deenie mirrored my movements, and I began to see my longing and my pain dancing in front of me. I kicked off my shoes and started to jump. It felt like flying.

Deenie was dancing an exalted cakewalk, grand and sassy, prancing with her knees high, and then abruptly she collapsed from the waist, though her feet kept dancing. She hung over her feet and let her backbone sway like seaweed in the tide. Her helplessness slowly grew into courage as her face led her up to a taller, wiser posture. She leapt victoriously across the barn and landed in a comical crouch. I followed her, and we circled each other with frog-like hops, our burning eyes locked, waiting for the impulse of the next moment. Every thing we did, we meant.

We were panting, and the dust we had kicked up was dancing in the doorway where the setting sun picked out each separate mote. A black shape loomed suddenly against the light. Deenie threw herself up onto the hay bales, and I stopped where I was, caught in place, my mind darkened by panic.

"What are you kids doing out here?" Her mother's voice was harsh as a seagull's, grainy and coarse.

Deenie said nothing.

"Git in the house, Jadeen!" her mother rasped, raising a threatening hand.

Deenie slid down from the hay and slipped past

her mother, who turned and followed her without even glancing at me. I stood up in the dark barn and felt my heart beat against my body, in my ears, my vision fading and flashing in the same convulsive rhythm. My legs and arms grew cool as the sweat evaporated, and I felt myself stiffening and frozen, cut loose from my ordinary life and associations, drifting.

Willard stepped into the barn. In panic, I ran through the wide doorway as far from his body as I could, grazing my arm on the rough wood in my flight. As I dashed past, he jumped sideways and gave a startled shout, and I realized he had not been coming to get me, boogy-man fashion. He had not known that I was there.

Walking home, I was alternately exhilarated and frightened. I smiled down at my dirty, trembling legs as they carried me gamely along. Passing the Flatwater City Library, I stopped suddenly on the sidewalk and swung my torso out and around the foundation of my right leg in a warm, fluid orbit. I tried to swing left, but I found the movement unexpectedly mechanical and jerky.

I tried again. My left leg was just not willing to be central, and my right leg couldn't give up control. By working in small circles, right and then left, always aware of my weight shifting from foot to foot, moving in progressively wider circles, I finally found a smooth symmetry that was effortless and yet required an intense concentration. I started home again, now in moonlight, stopping only once more to work out how a dog might dance and then to try to dance the cakewalk like Deenie just so I wouldn't forget.

I was thinking about dancing as I stepped onto our porch. In the instant when I touched the door, it flew open, I saw my mother's distraught face framed in the doorway, I felt an unexpected rush of love for her, and I realized I had left my shoes in the barn. She pulled me in and paused a moment, leaning on the closed door to look at me before she swooped down and enfolded me in a hug I returned with fervor.

"Don't you ever, ever, do that again," she said. And I said I never, ever would. Seeing her so close to tears made me cry as I tried to explain. She held me very close, and I clung to her as though returning after a long journey, improbably whole. We were startled out of our embrace by a dull thump on the door, and when we opened it together, there lay my dusty black-and-white saddle oxfords on the porch.

That night, as I huddled under my bedsheets, I held the flashlight under my chin and drew a red daisy, the same daisy I always drew, a small circle, then a series of petals, a short stem, and two leaves, on the white toe of one shoe and then the other. I filled in the petals with different colors and filled the white spaces on the heels with stars, hearts, and other doodles in other colors, at random, until there was no more room to fill. In the morning, my mother eyed my newly decorated shoes and shook her head, but said nothing.

My walk to school that morning was different than usual. My step was lighter, and I would have skipped, but I was too intent on watching my feet. When I arrived, the other little girls from all the grades gathered around me, impressed by my artwork and my nerve. The farm and town girls alike were drawn from the swing set and the tetherball games into the circle of admiration and new possibility that surrounded my shoes. By the next day, saddle oxfords would bloom in all the classrooms, with flowers, clowns and ponies of all colors, red lips and faces of princesses with yellow hair and blue eyes. Some of the girls sat down in the dirt then and there and started embellishing their own shoes, lending pens to each other and trading colors and squabbling just a little over who could have the red pen next.

I glanced up and saw Charisse standing alone at the top of the school steps, glaring down at us like a witch in her plain, black, undecoratable loafers. Her spell was finally broken.

David Fell
& Karen Rose

Because Mrs. Howarth had the worst cold she'd had in years and forgot to send the job announcement out until Good Friday, thus causing it to run while a large percentage of the population had escaped the city; because Mitzi Tegner took her new roommate's advice about dressing for the interview—"No really, wear the red one. It shows your boobs and sexy is what gets you hired, really!"; because Dr. Harrison was concerned about the possibility that he had gone entirely too far in discussing Henry Miller with an uncomfortable Heidi Wacker with his office door closed; because Dr. Rasmussen had been dreaming blissful, bread-scented dreams about his Danish grandmother for several nights running; because David Fell was distracted by the intense pain in his gut, which was not responding to home remedies or over-the-counter bromides, and so was unable to bring his usual incisive and humane intelligence to the process of evaluating applicants;

because Patty was informed rather than consulted about the hiring of her office assistant, much to her irritation; for all these reasons, Karen Rose Anderson became general dogsbody in the Department of American Studies, and so was in an ideal position to glean as much as possible from David Fell's death.

He was certainly kind to her, shaking her hand after the interview and saying "Nice to meet you, Karen" in a warm, resonant voice.

"Karen Rose," she had said. "I go by both names," and she blushed as though admitting something intimate, giving the impression that she was lying, although it was the honest truth.

"Karen Rose, then," David Fell had corrected himself with a smile and the slightest hint of a bow in her direction, a courtesy that deepened the rose on Karen Rose's cheek. As he turned away, the pocket of his smooth, blue shirt burst into flame, or so it seemed to Karen Rose. She looked away quickly. No one else seemed to notice, so she thought she might be mistaken. She often noticed things that other people didn't choose to remark on. She had learned to assume that there was no point in figuring things out. She thought that's what people meant by the phrase "just one of those things."

For example, on her Greyhound bus ride to the Bay Area, up from Manteca, she had seen a man pulled over on the side of the road, urinating into his car through the open door, the stream sparkling in the sunlight and making a shining pool on the seat. She couldn't think of an explanation and, because of the element of nastiness in the scene, she was doubly eager to put it out of her mind.

She couldn't actually remember a time when she hadn't seen those things. Her very earliest memory was when she was almost eleven and her uncle Ed had taken her home from the hospital. A man parked next to them pulled his sun visor down and a trout fell into his lap. Karen Rose saw it distinctly as Uncle Ed backed his old red truck carefully out of the parking place.

"That man had a fish," she said, or thought she said, but Uncle Ed didn't look at her or say anything, and so she decided it was either unwise or maybe even impossible to communicate about the things that seemed to happen. It might even be impolite, and she was a very polite little girl. From that time on, she tried to ignore anything that she wasn't sure was really happening or that other people chose not to notice, like David Fell's flaming pocket. Her smile was uneasy, and she hoped she was making a good impression.

Patty called her a week later to tell her she got the job—temporary, part-time office assistant. Karen Rose thanked her graciously and agreed to start work the next afternoon. Then she hung up and went back to frying some chicken for her dinner, the smell of salty grease soaking into the dark walls of her small apartment. She re-tied the strings of her hand-embroidered apron with a business-like smile. Her elaborately braided pale brown hair was wound around her head in an old-fashioned, old-world corona. The smile on her pale fleshy face was sweet and self-conscious.

"Young girls are so dreamy," Aunt Daisy used to say, herself a stringy, dreamless, Christian woman. Karen Rose still saw herself as being summed up in that sentence, though she was now twenty-seven. After Aunt Daisy died, gray and rigid in the county hospital bed, Aunt Belle, the black sheep, had been the only family Karen Rose had left to depend on.

"What shall I do now?" Karen Rose had wailed, stimulated by the drama and pathos of her bereaved condition.

"How the hell should I know?" snapped Aunt Belle, cigarette smoke pouring from between her purpled lips. "Get a job," she snorted, "get married, do whatever you damn well please."

Karen Rose ignored the bad words. She thought she should get married, but the only male in her experience was her second cousin, Angus, black-browed, smirking Angus, who had once reached under her skirt while they were watching TV and grabbed her between the legs so hard that she might have been bruised, though she was too modest to check. The pain was shocking, but the attention made her feel smooth and womanly, like an egg. She had thought that she might end up married to Angus, but he left to go to college in Lubbock and didn't come back.

Karen Rose knew she would be a good wife. She was pure and willing and a tireless cook. Even living alone, she cooked full meals every day of the week and sat down to a table set with care. On Saturdays, as she cleaned house all day, she cooked a pot of navy bean soup with ham hocks, served with boiled greens and sliced tomatoes. On Sundays, she cooked pot roast with carrots and potatoes, gravy, red jello salad with fruit cocktail, buttered rolls, and chocolate cake. On Mondays, meat loaf with tomato sauce, scalloped potatoes, green beans, and leftover cake. On Tuesdays, fried chicken with mashed potatoes and gravy, peas, coleslaw, and leftover jello salad. On Wednesdays she ate leftover roast with catsup, leftover mashed potatoes fried in patties, leftover vegetables, and apple cobbler. On Thursdays, she cooked macaroni and cheese and served it to herself with a tomato salad, baked beans, and brownies. All of this cooking took up much of her time, especially since she prided herself on cleaning up the last pot and pan before she bathed, slipped discreetly into her nightgown, and went to bed.

Sometimes she imagined Angus there, sharing her heavy, American dinners with her. It was easy to imagine him because she kept her eyes lowered modestly, enjoying his admiration. Her refrigerator was always crammed full of food, but she continued to cook as Aunt Daisy had cooked, and tsked indignantly over the waste when she was forced to throw old food away.

On Friday nights, after she had started working at the university, she washed and combed her long cumbersome hair and gathered it into a ponytail. Then she changed into her only pair of jeans and called out for a pizza. She felt delightfully irresponsible on Friday night; it was her teenage night. She ate pizza and drank Coke and read magazines, toying with her ponytail and slumping a little from her normal unnaturally stiff posture. Young girls are so dreamy.

Karen Rose enjoyed working for Patty. She filed and typed and made copies of things, even took detailed messages without too many errors. She played office and simpered a little as she worked. All of the instructors were nice to her, but she especially admired David Fell with his wild black hair and his green eyes. She worried that he wasn't getting enough to eat. She began to use him as her imaginary dinner partner, as though this would build up his imaginary health. She replaced Thursday's brownies with banana pudding, thinking that the milk would be good for him. She was not the only one who was worried about David Fell.

"Have you seen the doctor yet?" Patty asked him at least once a week. He laughed and called her "Little Mum," which annoyed her and made Karen Rose feel faint with envy. He was a tease, a flirt, a darling unmanageable man. He promised and he protested, but he always had an excuse, even as the lines in his graying face grew deeper and the occasional pain became chronic. When the chronic pain became acute enough, he broke down and called for an appointment. By the time the test results came back, he was desperate for relief and no longer laughing.

"I'm sorry to have bad news for you," the nervous doctor had told him. "You have a malignancy, a cancer."

"Of what?"

"Cancer of the pancreas. The scans came out very clear." He stopped and looked down at his big, clean hands. "It's pretty far advanced. You must have been in pain for months."

"Are we talking surgery here?" David asked, though he knew they weren't. "Chemo? Radiation?"

"I'm afraid not. There are therapies we use very successfully for symptomatic relief, but you've left it rather late."

"How long do I get?" He was beginning to shake, so

he looked down at his own slender hands, so familiar, so useful.

"Of course it's impossible to say for certain. Speculating, I would say four weeks. Not long, I'm afraid."

"You're not afraid," David said. "I'm afraid."

The doctor nodded. "I can check you into the hospital this afternoon," he said carefully. "There's a great deal we can do to make you more comfortable, but I'm afraid...I'm sorry."

"I need to think. I'll let you know." David was surprised to find how much he wanted to hit the doctor, leave him with injuries that would continue to throb when his own tortured body was painless, cold, and still. Remember me.

"You may think of other questions you have later. Please feel free to call me if anything comes up you need to talk about. Okay? I can give you a prescription for the pain, but there's a lot more we can do for you once you check in."

"I know," David said. "I just need to think."

"Is there anyone who could be with you at this time? A family member? Anyone we could call for you?"

"I'm on my way to talk with a friend. Thank you for your concern," David managed between teeth gritted with the effort to behave with dignity and to override the burning distress in his belly. His mouth tasted of bile and salt.

David Fell went straight to the temporary building that housed American Studies to argue with Patty, possibly for the last time. Karen Rose was standing at the copy machine, slowly and methodically feeding originals in and stacking copies on the small table next to the machine. David ignored her puppyish, wriggling greeting and grabbed Patty's arm, pulling her with him into Dr. Rasmussen's deserted office. Through the half-open door, Karen Rose could hear them talking, escalating to shouts. She tried to understand what was happening, but since she was also trying not to hear the bad words, she couldn't make any sense out of it. She heard David snarl, "Back off, Patty! Don't even start with me!"

"Why can't you let me help? Just be there for you, like another human being? To talk to? To cry with? Is that so awful, David, just to be human?"

"Don't you fucking nurture me, Patty!" David warned.

Karen Rose pictured Patty with her breast exposed, trying to put the nipple in David's mouth. She couldn't think that, so she went blank and cold, standing at the humming machine.

David was sorry, finally. He realized suddenly, as Patty stopped trying and just pleaded with her teary eyes, that he was fighting with her because she cared about him and had red hair. Mostly it was the hair. Just watching the indignation and passion in her made him feel alive. It was unfair. He was sorry. But he still meant to die his own way, without handholding or hushed, smugly righteous, maddeningly viable spectators.

"What about pain, David?" Patty wanted to know. "At the hospital they could make you more comfortable. A visiting nurse could give you injections for pain. You're going to need some help. I can't just let you die."

"You can't stop me, Patty. I wish you could." David was inspired at that moment with an idea that struck him as genius. "I'll have some help," he said, smiling. It isn't often that having a junkie for a nephew is an asset to a person, but when the person is dying anyway, a shot of heroin from an expert could be the very thing. He felt clever for having found an evasion of the kind-hearted, well-meaning mainstream. He would have an outlaw death, which struck him as much more respectable. Not angels but junk would carry him to Heaven.

"I'll be okay," he said. "My nephew, Steven, can come stay with me."

Patty relaxed visibly. "Let me know if you need anything at all," she said. "If you want to talk. If you want me to help. Anything, David, really."

"Thanks," he said. "Thanks but, after all, blood is thicker than water. Get Henry to take my film class."

Another minute to look at her suddenly dear face, and he was gone.

Patty sat in the still office remembering David until she heard a strange whimpering from the main room. It was Karen Rose, still standing at the copy machine, tears running down her face for the first time since she was almost eleven. Her plump arms felt icy cold to Patty's touch.

"What is it?" Karen Rose whispered. "Why was he yelling?"

"Come on, kiddo," said Patty, linking her arm in Karen Rose's. "Let's find a place in the sun to talk."

Patty left a note on the office door, "Closed for emergency," and led Karen Rose out to the little quad on the west side of the building. They sat close together on the stone bench, and Patty tried to explain.

"Can't he get some medicine?" Karen Rose asked. "Does he need a nurse? I can cook," she offered shyly.

"He doesn't want us to help him. Apparently, his nephew is going to come and stay with him."

"How will we know when he dies?"

"I guess the nephew will call the office. I don't really know, Karen Rose."

A big, muscular man in a jogging suit huffed by them, a darling white lamb's head sticking out of the brown paper shopping bag in the crook of his arm. Its little pink mouth opened and closed in time to the

45

runner's labored breathing.

"Did you see that?" Karen Rose asked, encouraged by Patty's kindness and closeness to attempt to resolve her own private mystery.

"Cute!" said Patty, and Karen Rose was alone and confused again.

In the days that followed before David actually died, Karen Rose spent the mornings sitting on the curb across the street and a few doors down from David's house. She didn't want to be a bother, but she wanted to pray for him and it seemed to her that being in the vicinity of the object of her prayer would make her prayers easier to answer, as though she could call God down and then point Him to the appropriate house. "Go! Heal! Amen."

She saw no sign of Steven because she went to work in the afternoon, when Steven and his friends came to check things out. Junkies need their morning sleep. Karen Rose continued to keep house as always on weekend afternoons. It felt good to launder and clean and cook after her vigil on the curb left her cramped and stiff. She cooked easily digestible soups and puddings and ate them with a virtuous air.

David was in intense pain, finding it hard to eat or sleep. His first jolt of heroin was pleasant enough, but the effect on his already weakened body brought his death sooner than the doctor had guessed. One afternoon only ten days after his diagnosis, he lay in a pool of sweat and vomit in his bed, weak and crying, in an agony that left him without personality, without self. In a momentary hiatus from the pain, he raised a puke-encrusted hand and draped it over the side of his bed, fishing wildly for the phone. He wanted to call Patty. He wanted to call for help. Unfortunately, the phone had been sold along with the microwave, the TV and stereo, his car and everything else salable that he owned. Poor David. Some things are thicker than blood. He left his arm hanging over the bed's edge and gave himself back to the pain.

As the sun went down at the end of the quiet street, Karen Rose came wandering down the sidewalk, drawn to her place of vigil by a strange feeling. She sat in the rosy sunset light, praying and drifting off, and when it was dark, she drew closer to the fascinating house where David lay. The doors and windows were all closed, and the bushes close around the house made it seem secret and protected. She daringly pushed herself in between the cool leaves and the cement foundation at the corner of the house, lying down in the dirt and cuddling around the rough surface as though it were a spouse or little sister.

"I will hold him," she thought mistily. "I will hold

him here with my…" Here she faltered, but went on bravely, "with my body." The wall felt warmer as she lay there, cool wind occasionally touching her face. She heard the neighbors walk out to their car and a laugh. The streetlights couldn't reach her where she lay. Nothing could reach her. She was young, healthy, and tired, and after a while she fell asleep, curled around David's house.

Inside he turned his face to one side and let the bile and thin mucus trickle onto his already filthy beard. He was not at peace, but he was more than ready to die.

At three in the morning, Karen Rose was disturbed by a cat passing by on his nightly rounds. Her first awareness was that the house still held in her embrace had grown cold.

"He's gone," she thought. "David has passed away." And then, with pride and awe, "I let him go." She crawled out of the little space where she had nested, incubating death, and walked to her apartment through the dark, quiet streets. Karen Rose slipped into her long flannel nightgown, brushed her teeth, brushed her heavy brown hair one hundred strokes, and slept the rest of the night in her own warm, ruffled bed. She dreamed of David Fell. He came to her in a white robe and smiled on her with divine, green eyes. "I will be with you always," he said. "I will be for you always. I will be of you always." He held out his arms to her, his wonderful eyes full of love and redemption, and she ran to him to bury herself in his soft, cloudy sleeves.

As Karen Rose started to stir and stretch and then plunged back down into her pillow, on Sunday morning at 7:34, in a gush of pain and fluid, David Fell finally managed to die by drowning.

Patty had been trying not to call David to see how he was doing, knowing that he didn't want her, didn't want help, not wanting to force him to accept help when he was too weak to resist. On Sunday morning at 10:00 am, she gave in and called. "His nephew can answer. He doesn't have to talk if he doesn't feel like it. I can't just leave it like this." She held her dachshund next to her on the couch and punched in David's number. It rang and rang.

"Maybe he went to the hospital, after all," she thought, and tried calling there to see. By 10:40, it was clear that he had not been admitted anywhere. She called David's number for the fourth time. There still was no answer. Patty was shaking, a delicate tremor that she didn't even try to control. She held her dog's warm, sleek body and breathed three deep breaths. Then she called 911.

Jarvis Handy, the big-faced emergency medical technician who answered the call, took pride in his ability to save lives and was annoyed by souls that got away from him. The case he was proudest of was a ninety-six-year-old woman. "Some people would just let her die. Hey," he liked to say, "she's a human being. She's got as much right to live as anybody else." She, a Mrs. Golderman, had slipped away quietly in the early morning, the time of day when she usually slipped quietly into consciousness, as though she had absentmindedly taken a wrong turn on a familiar walk. Her great-niece, Angela, not wanting to be alone with the body and not knowing who else to call, dialed 911.

Jarvis had not hesitated to shock Mrs. Golderman's frail, empty body back to life, racing her to the hospital in a horrifying, confusing welter of hellish red lights, screaming sirens and the ghastly faces of strangers. She died again the next evening, heavily sedated.

Nor was Jarvis at all reluctant to break down David's door; in fact, he took a certain amount of physical pleasure in doing so. To his disgust, however, David's body was cool and empty. His dead eyes were cast back into his head, as though he had been reaching for a death that had hovered teasingly behind him. Brown liquid gleamed dully in his half-open mouth and made a stripe down one yellow cheek. Saving lives made Jarvis feel heroic. Picking up dead bodies made him feel low-class and dirty, like a trash man.

"Junkie," he said to his partner, looking around at the gutted apartment, the vomit-crusted corpse, the blackened spoon and candle on the floor. "God, I hate junkies."

Karen Rose took the news calmly on Monday afternoon when Patty told her David was dead. She knew he was not really dead, that he would live on in her soul. She had felt the passing of his spirit and he had come especially to comfort her.

On her way home that evening, she noticed a fresh, plump, unbeating human heart lying in the litter basket as people passed by, apparently indifferent. Karen Rose averted her eyes quickly, but then with a jerk, she turned and walked stiffly back to the basket.

"David will protect me. David will show me the way," she thought. She forced herself to look a long time, and finally saw that what had seemed like a discarded heart was actually a faded, paint-splotched red sweatshirt, the glistening membrane effect caused by a stray sheet of crumpled plastic. Holding her breath, she touched it with one stubby finger; it was only a rag.

Smitty's Love Story

My sister's name is Copper Rose O'Hara. She is a psychotherapist and she lives in Beverly Hills. My brother's name is Kent Dupree O'Hara. He is a surgeon and he lives in Aspen, Colorado. My name is Jean Smith O'Hara Snopes. My friends usually end up calling me Smitty, for my middle name. I work at Pennymart and I still live in Tulsa, where I was born and raised.

I was born last, and my parents didn't seem to realize until after my birth that they already had one of each, boy and girl, as though there might be a third gender to complete the set. Or maybe my ordinary looks made it hard for my beauty queen mother to see me against the backdrop of my beautiful siblings.

"So you were the baby of the family?" a therapist once asked me, and I had to laugh.

"No," I said. "I was the goldfish."

My mother's parents, my Dupree grandparents from Atlanta, adored Copper. When they came to visit, they made over her with syrupy accents that suggested the bite of honey caught in the throat. They took pride in Copper's auburn-haired beauty, sending her vaguely antebellum clothes and magnolia-scented perfume for Christmas, birthdays, confirmation. My father's parents, my O'Hara grandparents from Chicago, adored Kent. Although Copper became discernibly more Irish when they came to visit us, it was blond, athletic Kent they took on trips and bought school clothes for.

There were no Smith grandparents from anywhere, and as near as I could tell, my middle name had been picked at random, possibly out of the phone book. I still shake my head over that one. I've raised three kids myself, and as far as they know, I love them all the same.

But my mother adored Kent, and my father adored Copper. It was a closed system, like chemical bonding. It wasn't the carefully balanced mobile that self-help gurus sometimes use to show how families can be thrown out of whack. It was more like a square with diagonal lines inside it. My mother and father were the top corners, my sister and brother the bottom corners. I was in the middle, the bonds of affection missing me altogether, if not crossing me out. The lines of affiliation had hardened into custom well before my parents absent-mindedly produced me, like something picked up from an impulse display next to the checkout counter. You get home with it and you can't remember what you were thinking. But maybe they needed a witness, an audience for their practiced perfection and their beautiful life. And I was a perfect witness, always admiring, always on the sidelines.

The Dupree grandparents, my mother's parents, sent Copper to Europe for a year and then to Stanford, where she seemed to major in succeeding and in psychology. The O'Hara grandparents sent Kent to Harvard, then UCLA, then Johns Hopkins to become a rich plastic surgeon rearranging the faces and flesh of rich people for a hefty price. I wandered out of high school into the same job I have now at Pennymart, and I'm glad to have it.

Years later, much too late, after I had earned my Ten-Year Service Award, after my father had given up his law practice to play golf, when he was hospitalized with his first big stroke, he made me lean down across his bedside tray table with its unlovely mess of used tissues and paper cups. He whispered into my ear that he had some cash put by to send me to beauty school, but not to tell my mother. My mother, who was standing right there, whisked me out into the hall and assured me that he was out of his mind. All that money had gone for remodeling the pool, putting in handrails all around for his physical therapy, the work completed just a few days before the next stroke brought him back to the hospital.

"There's nothing left in that account," she said. "He's losing his faculties." She said it like she was accusing me, or putting an end to the incessant demands she imagined me making. Her smile made it clear she was glad to disappoint. Not that I was really drawn to the idea of beauty school at that moment in my life. But that's the last conversation I had with my dad before he died, and possibly the best one ever, since it suggested that he was thinking about me, even if that was a sign of dementia as my mother had implied. He was thinking about me even though I wasn't there in front of him, demanding attention, even though I was not particularly thinking about him right then.

People like my ex-therapist suppose it means something to be the baby of the family, the soft center of the family circle, the last sweet sip of lemonade in the glass. Maybe it does for some people. But to me it meant invisibility and perpetual envy. I was the camera, framing and recording the carefully photogenic family moments, choreographed to showcase my very attractive siblings and reflect favorably on my still attractive parents. Now I am the scrapbook, the one who remembers.

I'm not making this up when I say I didn't count. My mother literally didn't count me when she numbered her offspring. I learned this when I was three, getting pretty good at counting myself, all the way to ten. Copper would have been a sophisticated seven-year-old. Kent at five had just started kindergarten, and I was alone in the house with my mother for the first time. It seemed like a situation of enormous romantic potential; I thought she might decide I had pretty hair and brush it and talk to me. She might tell me something private. She might even play with me a little. I stood with my baby doll, Hilda, under one arm, watching her talk on the phone, waiting for our moment now that the others were out of the way for once.

She said, "I guess I might as well go ahead and get out my painting equipment again, now that the kids are both in school." She was looking in my direction, through me at the wall behind me. It was fear I felt, rather than sadness. I hid under her bed. I imagined her calling me all over the house, "Jean, honey, where are you? Come to mommy!" but it was a long, still day and no one called. How could it have been all day? It couldn't have been. But I remember lying there with Hilda held close, studying the shapes made by the springs on the underside of the bed and not crying by thinking about the Holy Ghost, which I pictured as a grey cirrus cloud that hovered around the Holy Family at about waist level, silent and unperceived, but still holy. I liked thinking about the Holy Ghost when

I was little. When I heard the kids get home from school, I came out, but I left something there and I can still picture the pattern of the springs, and the longing I felt has haunted me most of my life.

I got tougher as I grew older, and I tried at times to force my parents, especially my father, into some kind of recognition, of me, of them, of the reality, dancing around like an empty sock puppet. It was hard at times to see what I had to lose. I asked my father which relative I was special to, in the absence of a third set of grandparents.

"I guess Aunt Jane, maybe," he said. I had never met Aunt Jane, who lived alone in Baltimore. Baltimore took on a flavor, a jazzy sound, became a name to conjure with. I supposed I might move there some day and do big city things with Aunt Jane. I imagined that someday she would send me something in the mail—something special and exotic and just for me. I waited for years until I eventually forgot about it. I finally met Aunt Jane at my father's funeral.

"You're not Copper," she said. "You will have to pardon me, I rather lost touch with your father after his marriage. What is your name again?" I had to laugh.

I think a more active personality could have caused some real trouble, spoiled the family story, or destroyed my parents' peace of mind. I didn't have the nerve. My little adolescent rebellions took the form of bad manners: uncombed hair, staring at company, eating my pie crust first, those and other peccadilloes which begged for attention without the risk of creating an actual crisis. Even my mother's distaste was preferable to being blanked out entirely. I wasn't up for suicide, fearful not so much of death, but that no one would care, or possibly even notice. This has been a recurring nightmare, being condemned to die in the electric chair with my family standing around wondering if there would be time to go out someplace nice for lunch after the execution. A therapist might interpret this as unconscious anxiety. Given my family, it's a reasonable scenario.

After I graduated from high school, not knowing what else to do, I wandered over to Pennymart and applied for a sales position. They accepted me, and I started the next day. Once I got used to the smell of cold polyester, it wasn't so bad. I worked mostly with Lillian, a Baptist minister's widow, and Georgette, who always dressed up like she might be going to church, even though we wore smocks over our street clothes so that customers could recognize us if they had questions. Lillian would offer to pray for you if you had some trouble, like needing a new transmission or a root canal, and I didn't mind having her in my corner. Georgette had a poodle she would show you pictures of and she knew more recipes for dip than anyone you ever met. We gave each other little cards for special occasions, or sometimes just to say hi, thinking of you, just hang in there. I liked that.

It was a big store, so most people just got to be friends with the other people in their own area, like I was in Household to start with. But one of the floaters, Louie, got to know everyone, and everyone liked him. He mostly worked in Automotive or Home Furnishing, but he did just as well in Children's Clothing or Toys. Everyone teased him because he was always driving a different old car, ones he would fix up and sell as a sideline. The thing about selling a car to someone you're likely to see everyday at work is that it better not fall apart too soon. Georgette drove a Dodge Dart she got from Louie, and she swore by it.

Louie was the kind of guy people tend to like because he seemed to notice how you were, and it mattered to him. He liked to give people nicknames— not offensive or anything, but names that made them feel good. It was like a hobby for him. He called Lillian "Legs," which she liked even though she was so religious. It made you notice that although she was shaped pretty much like a bag of potatoes, she really did have nice legs. He called Georgette "Daisy," which also seemed to fit because she was so fresh and clean all the time. Those names were easy to remember and safe to use, and they made us feel like a family.

I was new, so I didn't have a nickname yet, and I thought about it more than I should have. Louie was stocking my area one day when I first got to work, and he said, "Hey, City Girl! Welcome to the salt mines!" I don't know why that hurt my feelings, but it made me feel like I didn't belong there with all those country-style people. He saw that in my face, I guess, because he got very serious and held out his hand, which I was happy to take.

"Hi!" he said. "Let me introduce myself properly. My name is Louis Warren Snopes. People call me Louie. And you are...?"

I shook his warm hand, and I said, "I'm Jean Smith O'Hara. Nice to meet you."

"Extremely nice to meet you, Smitty." And he always called me Smitty after that, and so did everyone else. I don't know why it pleased me so much, unless maybe it took the sting out of the generic Smithness that made me such an outsider in my own family and turned Smith into something worth having. Smitty was affectionate. It made me feel cute, and it brought me in.

After I got my job and moved out of my parents' house, things with my family shifted around a little. I used to see Kent and his wife and two girls when they were visiting for the holidays, but after the first year, I started working overtime at the store all through the season, up to midnight on Christmas Eve when I could. Then I might swing over in the morning and eat a cookie or two with the family, watch the kids open presents that I can promise you did not come from Pennymart, but after a while I stopped doing even that. Kent and I exchanged Christmas cards, mine from the discount bin from the previous year-end sale, his complete with a lovely family portrait taken in his lovely home. That was about what Kent and I had going right there. Once both of our parents were gone, one to the best cemetery in Tulsa, one to a condo in New Orleans, the three of us, the princess, the prince and the caboose, as I think of it, never got together. There was nothing to talk about, at least not to each other.

But Copper still seemed to have a use for me. She had always been too busy to come back to Tulsa for Christmas, and she didn't have any kids to show off anyway, so she just called from whatever exotic place she was visiting—Martinique, the Riviera, Tahiti. She would call me once in a while when it wasn't even Christmas, just to tell me how she was and who was in love with her and where they were going next, but whenever I made the effort to call her, it went to voicemail and ended there.

"Just calling to say hi," I would say. "Hi!" And I guess it's true, that doesn't really call for a response.

Kent became irrelevant to me, but Copper, the

beautiful sister, was still tricky, even after years of bad dreams, therapy, and self-help books. After all, if she hadn't been there, there might have been a space for me, and I might have seemed more important without her stunning example to be compared to. I think for me she was like a locked door. Everything good was on the other side of her, and I wasn't often invited in and I couldn't get past her. Ever since I can remember, I wanted her to discover me and take care of me, look at me, touch me, make me part of her so I could be beautiful, successful, and whatever else that was she had a corner on. Magic, maybe, or voodoo. I was grateful and eager to accept anything she offered me: contact, advice, cast-off clothing, though being three inches shorter than her, the clothes almost never fit right. I would hang them up with the others, thinking I'd go to a tailor and get them altered, but who can afford that?

When Copper was first setting up her practice in Beverly Hills, she sent me plane fare to come visit her and help out. I took my whole two weeks of vacation to go. I was electrified, like I was finally her sister. I went, thinking she might practice a little psychoanalysis on me, make me confident and assertive. Maybe she'd fix me up, like a makeover. I pictured us sitting in front of a mirror side by side, talking about my face. What would bring out my beautiful eyes, cheekbones, stuff like that. I imagined double dating at some fancy restaurant in Hollywood, where movie stars are as thick as dandelions. I had some big ideas.

Instead, we spent long days shopping for furniture and carpeting and decor, stuff for the walls of her new office, which had to be painted the exactly right shade of beige, with a name that sounded like a perfume or a lipstick, Aurora Desert or something like that. I was often installed in the empty, newly painted space, inhaling paint fumes, reading the funny papers, and doing the crossword, to wait for deliveries of her lavish purchases. An artist she said was a former lover made her a collage for the focal point, a really enormous thing she planned to put on the office wall. It was made of long, convoluted copper tubing, big, bigger than a tuba, intertwined with strips of rose satin fabric bunched up like used bed sheets, but gorgeous, classy. When the two delivery guys muscled it through the door, I had to laugh. It was like waving her own enormous, unassailable ego at her poor insecure patients—Copper Rose, the belle of Bedlam. It made me want to meet the artist.

She was particularly worried about one low-income patient she had taken on pro bono—that he would soil the desert taupe couch and leave dirty footprints on her brand-new winter white carpet. I don't know why she agreed to work with him in the first place. She didn't seem to like him and she said he had no inner life. When I saw him, the first patient to stew in the finished waiting room, he sat unmoving on her couch, folded arms defending his chest, legs twisted around each other an extra turn, his eyes blank with the pain and distress of road kill after impact, before release. I didn't try to make conversation with him. I just sat quiet and tried to breathe for the both of us. It looked to me like inner life was probably the only kind he would be capable of conducting. I think what Copper meant had to do with appreciating good wine and fine art.

After the flight home to Tulsa, having spent two weeks in Copper's luxurious townhouse, I walked into my grubby apartment, with the pathetic art posters taped to the walls to cover the peeling green paint, and I felt hurt all over. It wasn't just my feelings. My head ached, my muscles ached, and I began to cough that night, a wracking cough that shook me like a rag. I felt as though I could only safely breathe by sipping the air into a small pocket at the back of my nose, because if I breathed any deeper, the cough was back, and it wouldn't stop. The next day, the doctor told me I had walking pneumonia, and to lie down before I fell down.

I called in to tell Lillian I was sick and spent the next three days hanging around my cluttered place, napping, watching stupid TV shows, and trying to move without jarring my lungs, moving less and less. By the fourth day, I had got to the point where I wasn't sure I would even notice, let alone care, if I died. My depressing little apartment was littered with cans, bread wrappers, used tea bags, and piles of dirty dishes. I had been well enough to get things dirty, but not well enough to clean anything up. It was raining and cold, and I lay on my plain beige couch and watched the rain slide down the window. Then I'd sleep for a minute or two, and then open my aching eyes to see the same gray square of sky.

And then Louie called. He hadn't seen me at the store, so he bothered to call and see if I was okay. Which I wasn't. I don't know what it was I said, but he came over to my place right away. I saw his big, round face in the window the next time I opened my eyes. I staggered to the front door and let him in, then collapsed on the couch again. I was sorry I was presenting such a sad, unappetizing picture, but I couldn't help it. He tsked and shook his head, and the tears started running down my cheeks into my ears. He plumped my pillow and brought me a clean blanket out of the linen closet. He brought me tea and fed it to me, blowing onto each spoonful of hot liquid like a flute player. He brushed my hair and washed my face, and I closed my eyes and listened to him as he moved around the apartment.

Maybe it was the fever, but I could hear like a fox, like a coyote. I heard the water run in the sink, the bubbles popping in the suds. I heard tiny sounds I had only felt before, like the ping of stubborn dried-on bits of food leaving the plates. I could hear the texture of the dishrag scraping against the counter, and the husky sweep of the broom, smooth and then snagged by things that had dried on the floor. I heard his breath expelled as he bent over and the sweep of each broom straw against the metal dustpan.

I could hear the hesitation in his movements when he looked around the unfamiliar kitchen for where things went or came from, and heard him resume his actions when he thought of where to look. The sleeves that were rolled up on his arms brushed against the body of his shirt with a whisper. I could picture him entirely as I lay there motionless with my eyes closed. I could smell his warm body and soap and steam. I heard him pull down the saucepan from the top shelf, catching the loose lid that always slid off, keeping it from clattering onto the floor. I heard him open the cabinet over the stove, and suck on his teeth as he studied the contents. The soup can scraped against the shelf and the can opener crunched as it bit down, then circled the lid. He pulled it off with a faint "tink" and poured the contents into the pan. It sounded lumpy— chicken noodle then, not tomato. And after the puff of the burner coming on, I began to smell it as well.

I tried to thank him, but he got embarrassed and said we'd talk when I got well.

"No," I said, "no one has ever been this nice to me in my whole life," and then I felt scared that I had said too much, sounded crazy or needy, which God knows I am. But I hoped he might not think I meant it literally, which of course I did.

He kissed me on the forehead and said, "Just get well, Smitty. I'll be around." By the time he left that evening after feeding me soup and finding a clean nightgown for me and tucking me into a clean bed, I was feeling much, much better, about everything. This is my love story.

Copper called me the morning after Louie was there, and I told her all he'd done. I thought it was the most magic thing that had ever happened, and I thought she would be impressed. It wasn't a big hunk of art like she got, but it was a really big deal to me.

First she said, "Is he gay or something?" and I said I was pretty sure not. Then she said, "Oh God, Jean, watch out! You're just the type to fall for that kind of symbolic mothering."

I believed her, maybe because I wanted Louie so bad that I didn't know what to believe, maybe because I was partly still under her spell. I rehearsed a conversation with him over and over in my mind.

When he showed up the next day, this time with a bag of groceries, I tried to have the conversation I had planned. I hadn't learned yet that this never works.

"I need to talk to you about yesterday," I said. I wanted to sound smart and together like Copper, but I must have overdone it. Louie looked apprehensive. "I'm afraid that I am very vulnerable to what a person might call symbolic mothering."

Louie drew back, his brown eyes hurt and puzzled. "Symbolic, my heinie!" he said. "If that was mothering, which I doubt, it was about as real as it could be!" He stuffed his hands in his back pockets. "Hey, I was just trying to help out. You want me to leave you alone, Smitty, you can just say so. You don't have to dress it up."

I started to cry, said I was sorry, I didn't mean it, it was just what my sister said. I was so scared I was probably not making much sense, but I let him know that I most definitely did not want him to leave me alone, not then and not ever. He wrapped his arms around me and rocked me and kissed my hair and my face, saying sweet things that made me about as happy as I'd ever been, and I found that I had a strong desire and, never mind the pneumonia, enough energy to make love with him. That was a long time ago, but I still think about it sometimes, because it's when my life began in earnest.

* * *

My mother died last week, and we'll all go down for the funeral. It has been years since she moved back to New Orleans "to be with family," she said, meaning cousins, I guess, since she was an only child and her parents were long gone by that time. I think really she just wanted to get old and fall apart in private, having run out of beauty but still having plenty of pride left. It seems like she withdrew from the party while she could still make a gracious exit. The last thing she wanted was a witness. After she moved, I tried to get her new phone number from Copper, but evidently she didn't have one. She was rapidly growing too deaf to get much use out of a telephone. That was the story. So I wrote proposing a quick visit to see her, bringing Louie and the kids, whom she had never met. She wrote back by return mail, saying that her engagements were such that it would be best to put the visit off until another time. She would let me know when it would be more convenient to entertain guests. And that was the end of that.

Knowing that her life is over makes me think about myself. When I picture what my life has been, this is the image that comes to me: me in the driver's seat of Louie's latest junker, pushing on the brake pedal, or turning the ignition key, or pushing on the accelerator, while he says "Okay. Stop. Okay. Stop. Try it again.

Stop." I sat here when I was so pregnant I could barely fit behind the wheel. I sat here and nursed my babies, pushing pedals, turning the key, stopping.

And now, as I sit here again tonight, this time in an '87 Camry, waiting for instructions, I picture my mother as I saw her so often, posed at her maple secretary, writing thank-you notes with delicate, even strokes on thick, creamy notepaper. Her glossy chestnut hair is drawn back into a knot at the neck, her stockinged legs held together at the knee and canted slightly sideways. One of her beautifully shod feet is tucked behind the other. I can see her, and I try to imagine her breath, her heartbeat, but all I can hear is the scratch of the pen as she inscribes her thanks, compliments, and respects.

"Okay," Louie says. I can't remember if okay means push or let go.

"Okay," he repeats, craning his head around the open hood. We see each other through the windshield. His forehead is wrinkled with concern and his cheek is anointed with dirty oil.

"Are you okay?" he asks me, and I nod.

"Okay," he says. "Just hold the accelerator down till I say to let go. Okay?"

"Okay," I say.

"Okay," he says again, and I hold the accelerator down till he says to let go.

71

Rhoda Welkin

Rhoda Hale was born with blue feet. Circulation problem, quite usual in newborns. All of the life, love, and joy in the child collected in her feet instead of circulating through her body. Her parents, like many adults in the fifties, believed that children, just like animals, didn't really feel anything, and yet strangely, they also believed that their major task in rearing Rhoda to adulthood was to eliminate any extremes of emotion that might inconvenience them or others. Their own range of passion ran from mild pleasure to mild displeasure. Things were either nice or not very nice. There were no arias sung in the Hale household.

Most infants shriek and kick the circulation back into their blue feet, but Baby Rhoda grumbled instead of shrieking, wriggled instead of kicking, and as a result, her feet stayed blue, or at least bluish. She didn't grow up to dance or run marathons or sell shoes or paint toenails, though other babies like her certainly did. It wasn't like that for Rhoda. Her feet were swollen and painful. She didn't love anyone or have fun, and of course she was resentful. Whenever things went wrong and people disappointed her, she felt a grim satisfaction. The grief sank down into her congested feet and anchored her more firmly than ever. She dreamed of flying almost every night, but she never remembered her dreams.

The greatest sensual satisfaction of her young life had been the summer of her seventh year—not the cows or the steamy green grass, but the way her bare feet were eased by the hot sidewalk in downtown Flatwater where her grandpa owned the movie theater. Not the movies, which she couldn't remember, but the grit of popcorn kernels underfoot—sticky splashed soda that said other people had lived where she was sitting, her dull eyes focused on the big screen, her jaws methodically demolishing whatever she put in her mouth, malted milk balls, licorice, popcorn. She expected nothing for herself beyond that covert, ground-level experience and yet she was constantly disappointed.

At first, the other children she went to school with tolerated her, but by the third grade she had been labeled and cast out, though she didn't seem to care. On a birthday trip to the zoo, Eppie Benson's father had been taken aback by her heavy, contemptuous reaction to everything from the apes to the zebras. Rhoda didn't see what all the fuss was about—they were just animals standing around. They weren't doing anything special. The snack bar only had two flavors of ice cream. It was hot. Everything was too crowded. Mr. Benson started calling her Killjoy and calling her over to show her things, just to get her consistently cranky reaction. It would make a better story that way.

Rhoda liked the attention and continued to give him her baleful critique of the whole zoo experience. You couldn't even see the baby chimp. The lions were just sleeping. The polar bears got to cool off in the water, but she had to stand around getting hot. By the end of the excursion, the other girls had picked up the name and called her Killjoy until he was sorry he had started the teasing, but Rhoda didn't care what they said. Killjoy sounded like they were a little afraid of her, and she kind of liked that.

Rhoda was scornful of pretty young women, of course, even when she herself was still young and healthy enough. Oh sure, while you're young it's all champagne and feathers. But have a baby, get a few wrinkles, and they push you out into the gutter, wait and see. Champagne and feathers went by quickly in Rhoda's thought, too exciting to hold on to, but it was as close as she came to poetry.

Rhoda Hale met Albert Welkin when she was thirty-three. He was quite a bit older, unmarried, and had a little video place where she sometimes rented videos for her quiet weekends. He was attracted to her grouchy tone; it struck him as sultry, adult, even x-rated.

She was attracted to the idea of being married, thinking that perhaps she could quit her job at the bank and stay home and have kids. Not that she wanted them, but they were the next step in the life course that she was on, the silver highway that slid off into the distance, smaller and smaller, until it winked out altogether.

The Hales came to their daughter's wedding and commented on how nice everything was and what a nice man Albert was. Rhoda's dress, an ill-advised beige, brought out the incipient dissatisfaction wrinkles around her mouth. Albert noticed only the fullness of her bodice, how large and delicious her breasts looked behind the beige lace. Rhoda stumped down the aisle on aching feet in shoes dyed to match her dress with straps making parallel red indentations in her ankles even as she said I do, her tone suggesting that the preacher had somehow implied that she didn't.

The marriage settled down to a drab intimacy after the first few months. They bought a small house in a bad neighborhood and Rhoda kept her job in order to help pay for it. She grew used to Albert, the smell of his hair, the dark sheen of his eyes, his propensity to leave his glasses in the windowsill. At first when she looked at his hairy chest, she saw it as large and manly. After a while, she began to see the pale, loose flesh under the sprouting black hair as defining the shape of his body and his general inadequacy as a husband. Sex was a chore to Rhoda, but one she secretly enjoyed. Not that she experienced orgasm—but she liked the way Albert huffed and rubbed against her, she liked the way he moaned when he came. Her feet twitched a little when he squeezed her broad bottom.

Once in a while, when they were watching TV together in the evening, he would reach over and rub her feet, as he remembered his father doing to his mother in the dark TV-lit living room of his childhood. Rhoda found it unnervingly, almost unbearably, pleasurable. She always pulled her feet away before she made a fool of herself. Since Albert was focused on the blue TV screen, he missed the flush of sensuality that warmed her face.

Rhoda didn't like the way she felt about Albert, and as a result she felt that Albert was not doing what he should. She felt covertly attracted to his flaccid pink nipples, and she was afraid that she was queer in some way for feeling this fascination. She didn't think men should have nipples; she felt men's nipples should be decently ignored. She also wanted to lick them till they stood up like little beaded flowers and the conflict between what she thought and what she wanted made her hard to get along with. Whenever he went around the house without his shirt, she grumbled at him repressively to for God's sake quit slopping around the house half-naked.

The thing that Albert did that bothered her the most was his wasting time on Mrs. Haggerty, two doors over. She was just an old lady, not strictly a lady, if you asked Rhoda. Her house smelled like mothballs and cookies and dust, and her ginger tomcat dug holes for his crap in Rhoda's yard. After Rhoda had made it clear as glass that she didn't want to take in a movie or go out for drinks on Albert's one evening off, Albert had started going over there, taking the cribbage board his grandfather had left to him and a deck of cards that said "Coca-Cola" on the back.

"I don't know why you mess with her," Rhoda complained. "She's not even all that clean. And God knows she's unpleasant."

"It's okay, Rhoda," Albert would mumble. "She's lonely, and I don't have anyone else to play with."

"Like I have time to waste with an idiot game like that," Rhoda snorted. "Huh! Fat chance, Mr. Albert Do-Gooder!"

Sometimes he took Mrs. Haggerty vegetables or flowers from his garden, where he spent happy morning hours before the shop opened digging and humming old show tunes. His garden was another point of contention with Rhoda, who was suspicious of food that wasn't wrapped in plastic and paid for with cash. She supposed that the vegetables had cat crap in them. Rhoda was not a comfortable woman to live with, but Albert was used to grumbling. To him, it was the background buzz of domestic comfort and family life. It filled the silence that children would have filled, if they had come.

No one was more surprised than Rhoda when Albert simply dropped dead one night, out in his precious garden looking up at the sky for Jupiter, which the weatherman on Channel 7 had said was visible just to the north of Orion. Albert's heart spasmed and he fell, thinking as he went down that he had been shot, in his last moment, confusing his own life with the life he saw in the movies. Rhoda was inside on the couch reading a magazine article about making the most of your living room. She turned the pages scornfully, shaking her head from time to time, her mouth pursed in bitterness.

Her only thought when she found him several hours later was that it was the kind of thing that always happened to her, and that he should have taken better care of himself or been younger. His mouth hung open in a way that embarrassed her, so she covered him with an old blanket while she waited for the ambulance.

"What kind of man was Albert?" The minister she

called to do the service had leaned forward and gazed at her.

Rhoda set her mouth stubbornly. Can't he just do the funeral?

"Many families, I find, prefer to have the service personalized to celebrate the life of the loved one. For example, Mrs. Welkin, what hobbies or activities was Albert involved in?"

Rhoda's mind was blank except for a nagging feeling that her time was being wasted. "He liked cats," she admitted.

Albert was buried in a cemetery she hadn't known existed, and the sun had been too hot, the preacher's voice too soft, and a loud Mexican funeral a few plots over had distracted and annoyed her. Why did they have to cry so loud? She wondered if Albert would have liked a T-shirt with his face on it handed out to the three mourners who waited around his coffin for the burial to be over. But you would have to buy them in bulk to get any kind of discount.

She left the graveyard and drove home alone, wanting nothing more than to get off her feet. She walked up the long, straight sidewalk to the brown front door, where a blank mat welcomed her only by implication.

She closed the door behind her, dropped her purse, and dropped herself into Albert's recliner, which creaked harshly as it dropped back—a different creak, she thought, than when Albert had leaned back—sharper, more pained, as though Rhoda's push back was unexpectedly forceful.

She could smell Albert, especially when she turned her face into the headrest and breathed in. Albert molecules made of Albert. At the other end of the chair, her feet were tingling as though they were filled with sparkles or butterflies. She looked down and saw how cleverly her feet, no longer sore, were designed, how beautifully her foot flowed into her ankle. More like a hand than a hoof. The feeling was unsettling. She sat in silence until the refrigerator cycled off, letting her sense of herself include the deeper silence left behind. There was an aching constriction in her throat, a pressure she resisted and tried not to be aware of and longed to express.

Rhoda wrenched the chair to upright. "How do I quit thinking? What," she thought with a gaping sense of loss—"what was I doing before?" She pushed away to go to the bathroom—that's real enough. She peeled down her pants as she sat and left them in a pile at the foot of the toilet, and after she had peed, she looked down at them. "Do I always do that?" Is that how Albert knew her? On the white sink, next to the coldwater faucet with a few blobs of paint that had always been there—sloppy work, why can't they clean up after themselves—she saw a tiny black fiber, an eyelash, Albert's eyelash.

Using the tweezers, she deposited the eyelash carefully into an empty metal band-aid box she found in the trash. Moving around the house on swift feet, she collected the bits and pieces of Albert that were left—dandruff and the black hairs from his brush, a toenail clipping, used floss—the peppermint kind he liked—a used band-aid from when he had slashed his thumb on a thorn from one of his favorite roses. When her collection seemed complete, she set the band-aid box in the seat of Albert's recliner and called the doctor. "My feet are tingling," she told the appointment nurse. She almost said they were sparkling.

Her doctor couldn't explain what was happening. "People handle grief in different ways," he had said, nodding his head wisely. "Grief handles people in different ways," she paraphrased in her head, but she thanked him for his help. She was entranced by the soft brown of his hair and the soft, clean smell of his hands. For an instant, she wanted to lean over and smooth her face against them. She hurried out of his office, horrified by her impulse, but simultaneously aware of the smooth, sweet movement of her hips and the leftover breakfast taste of raspberries on her warm lips.

Her fellow workers at the bank wondered what

had happened to her, whispered among themselves that she must be having an affair. Shocking so soon after her husband had passed away, but then people handle grief in different ways. Rhoda began to dress differently, shopping for unexpected blues and misty greens, hot red and black, purple swirled with indigo. She felt like a fool, but was drawn to the sheer visual sensations of looking down at her body and seeing the colors and textures wrapped around her, enfolding her breasts and blanketing her thighs. She had to buy all new shoes; the old healthy shoes she had worn before seemed to be stretched out to flaccid rags. She replaced them with light, stylish sandals and colorful flats. She danced when she was alone, wondering at the same time if she was losing her mind.

She couldn't sleep at night for wanting Albert, wanting him to touch and to make love with, wanting to swallow him, to draw him into her love-dazzled body and drown. She masturbated, clumsily at first, and then with a deep passion. She believed it was a neurotic thing to do, but that after she adjusted to widowhood, she would naturally calm down. In the meantime, she developed an abidingly intimate relationship with every erotic sensation and nerve-rich spot on and in her body.

After a month of hot, passionate nights alone, sleepless and driven, she decided to visit one of the bars downtown, thinking that a drink would calm her down, that the social atmosphere would meet some of the needs that were ruining her nights. She was looking to get laid. She slipped out quietly, carefully not glancing at the recliner where Albert's box sat.

She was shy and stiff with the men who approached her, most of them no longer young, most of them uninhibited by drink, some incapacitated, but after the first few heart-stopping, clumsy encounters, she quit thinking about what she was doing and just did it. Often the men would take her out to their cars or their cheesy apartments; once or twice she pulled up her dress in the dark alley behind the bar for the stranger to enter her, pushing her against the grimy wall and giving her the pulsing pleasure she was seeking. She felt tender toward these men, the soft flesh of the inside of their arms, the sun-creased brown leather of their necks. For the most part they were rough and awkward, but she only smiled and guided their hard or half-hard penises through the tangle of her pubic hair and into the space that longed for them.

Rhoda tried not to go to the same bar too many times. She was afraid of being a regular. She didn't want to be talked about, so she never told her real name to her partners and she avoided the bars in the neighborhood of the bank. She worried about getting AIDS as she put on her perfume and lipstick, making a moist purple plum of her wide mouth. She was going to go again, no matter what she said to herself. She wasn't listening; she was strangely alive and joyful, even in the grimy, sad alleyways and the junky backseats of cars.

The last partner she took from the bars was a burly fellow who invited her home with him, opened the car door for her, and laughed at her jokes on the way there. His hands felt warm on her shoulders as he walked with her up the driveway. His house was neat, not like the depressed mobile homes and roachy apartments she had been to with other men. It was small, made up of one room that served as kitchen, sitting room and bedroom, but everything was tidy and organized.

He stood by the blue kitchen table, and she could see that he had an erection making a point in the khaki fabric of his pants. She looked down to unbutton her blouse, flattered by his desire and eager to touch him. Out of the corner of her eye, she saw him raise his hand, but the hard, slow blow to the side of her head caught her unprepared. She held her face where his hand had slapped her, looked up sideways at him from the crouch she had been knocked into. He was smiling at her, shaking his head.

"Hey, I didn't say take off your blouse, now did I?" he chided her. "You're going to do just what I say, little sister, or you're going to get hurt. Understand?"

She nodded, still holding her face. She was afraid: she could feel the fear trembling through her body, the needle points of adrenaline prickling in her hands and feet. "This is not right," she thought. He saw her look toward the door, and laughed delightedly.

"The door's locked, sweetheart. I have the key and I have you. Now, hadn't you better button up before you get hurt?"

She fumbled the buttons and buttonholes together, her eyes fastened on his.

"Good girl," he said, seating himself on the kitchen chair. "Now take off your shirt, girlie, I'm going to play with your tits."

She did everything he said to do, shaking and alert.

There was nothing he told her to do that she would not have been willing to do. He squeezed her breasts and sucked on her nipples and then ordered her clothes off. She stood naked, and he pulled his penis out of his pants and motioned her to give him a blowjob.

"Do it nice, little sister," he said, and tangled his fist in her hair to hold her down. He tasted sweet and salty, felt warm to her cold lips. Before he came, he pulled her head up and pushed her down on the bed. He kept his heavy hand on her throat, leaning there as casually as he might rest against the warm hood of a truck. He pushed into her and stroked up and down, his face red and sweaty, until he came, collapsing briefly onto her and then rolling over.

"Get out," he said. "I'm through with you." He turned his back and appeared to fall asleep there on the bed.

She grabbed her clothes and yanked them on, afraid he would wake up, that it was a trick.

"It's not really locked," he added sleepily, snorting a little laugh into the pillow. She ran.

Monday morning at the bank, Rhoda's face showed no mark of her experience on the skin; her eyes were clear and sad, luminous and illuminating. Her vivid flesh seemed to pulse against the drabness of the walls, the desks, the money. The other tellers sensed that she had changed again and felt drawn to speak with her, even to touch her arm, to smile and perhaps be smiled at by her. An aura of tenderness and compassion made the air in the bank rosy. Customers were satisfied.

On the third day after the assault, Rhoda rose from her bed and knew. She felt as though the mail she had been waiting for had been delivered and was there on the pillow next to hers. She went on through her routine of coffee, cereal, dishes in dishwasher, with her mind a little blank, or at least so it seemed after the crowd of impressions and feelings that had been with her since her last night out. The new silence in her head was very satisfying after the buzz she'd been living with. She sat in Albert's chair, holding his remains in her lap. He was the one she wanted to talk to. Because it seemed important, she spoke aloud.

"It's not that he hit me. I've hurt myself worse tripping over a rake in the back yard. I won't go out like that again, so I'm not afraid another man will hurt me worse. No, Albert, it's the meanness." Her voice shook and then steadied. "It's the damn old meanness—that's what it is." She rocked a little. "It was the meanness just to be mean, pleasure-hating, joy-killing meanness, that's what it was." She treasured Albert against her heart, and cried. Meanness was something she knew. It seemed like it might be another way of saying Rhoda, and that made her sobs deeper, almost like shouts. Her life appeared to her, not in separate pictures, but in total, the whole dismal, wasted length of it, uncelebrated, unintended, and random. It was not so much sad as soulless and shallow, and she longed for something, a chance to be different.

She blew her nose and, dressed in Albert's old overalls, she went out into the overgrown garden and began to pull weeds, feeling the way different roots held onto the dirt, enjoying the weeds that came out clean, and using a dandelion digger to tease out the others. She made a pile of the weeds behind her as she worked her way from the house to the wall, plunging into the earth and making room for Albert. She was surprised at how hard it was to be comfortable, kneeling or stooping or sitting, and also how hard it was to stop. Crying, but just a little, she buried Albert in his garden.

When it grew dark, she cleaned up and dressed again, this time in jeans and a Return of the Jedi T-shirt she had bought for Albert in the wrong size and never bothered to exchange. It felt comforting. After a supper of scrambled eggs and toast, she hunted for the cribbage board and the cards, went two houses down, and knocked on the shabby green door.

Mrs. Haggerty stuck her stringy-haired gray head out the door, peering short-sightedly around the chain. The one pale eye that was visible looked like a grape on a plate.

"What the hell do you want?" She blinked in the glare of the porch light.

Rhoda held up the cribbage board and waggled it back and forth invitingly.

"I suppose you think you can beat me, hunh?" said Mrs. Haggerty. And under her breath, she added, "Sorry about Albert." The door closed and then opened wide.

"I don't expect to win," said Rhoda. "I've never played before, so you'll have to teach me."

"Well, come in, then, don't let the moths in. All I

have in the house for a snack is saltines," she warned.

"Sounds delicious," said Rhoda. She went in and they sat down together at the rickety, stained card table to play while Ginger Tom watched from the third chair.

Mary Jesus

When Melody told me what her sister was up to, I was flabbergasted. For one thing, I had never thought of Carrie as a spiritual seeker. I knew she was dissatisfied with her job at the auto parts store, dissatisfied with her friends and her life generally, but I just never expected her to go that far afield. I didn't even know she was Catholic.

My daughters hadn't ever been very close. Like my twin Nancy and me, they were just littermates, more trouble to raise, but no identical cuteness factor to mitigate the slog, no secret language, no eerie bond connecting them. So I would have thought she would tell me or her dad instead of Melody before running off to Mexico, certainly before taking a vow of silence, although it's not like she speaks Spanish anyway.

"There's a website," Melody told me, as though that explained anything. "It's a real thing."

"Cults have websites too," I said. "What was she thinking?"

Melody stubbed out her cigarette and gave me a

shrug.

I don't understand my daughters. My two girls, now twenty-three, seem mostly depressed, though whenever I mentioned this, thinking that a diagnosis is halfway to a cure, a hopeful step in the right direction, they sighed and shrugged and looked away. When I was their age, I was exuberant, wildly excited about finally being an adult, off the leash at last. I ran around taking drugs and sleeping with beautiful bearded boys, writing songs and poems and dancing in the rain, dancing around fires, dancing wherever there was music, and there was music everywhere. We cared about everything in those days.

"That was then, Mom," my daughters like to say. "It's now now." And they look away and take another drag on a cigarette or paw listlessly through a stack of junk mail or find some other way to express how boring everything is. So I was encouraged in a way by the amount of initiative Carrie had shown, though still bewildered.

"Some guy she met told her about it," Melody said. She lit another cigarette and continued sorting the kids' laundry, most of which was an unhealthy grayish pink color. My grandchildren, Kyla and Barry, dressed like orphans in clothes you wouldn't even give to Goodwill, but Melody says they don't care. They just get dirty again.

"I guess she thought it sounded cool." Melody's phone started a drumbeat, and she picked it up and starting pushing buttons. "It's Matt," she explained, without looking up.

It sounded way uncool to me, and I felt the cold panic I had felt on the few occasions when I mislaid one of my girls, like the time Marcie Prentiss, like an idiot, had her teenage son do her carpool pick-up after swimming lessons, and he had come home one girl short. I drove to the Y with my heart thumping, Melody whining in the backseat about missing that Sponge Bob show, and rounded the last corner to find Carrie waiting patiently on the sidewalk, her pink purse over one shoulder, blonde hair dried into chlorinated strings, gym bag held in one hand, ready for departure. I jumped out of the car to envelop her in a hug, wanting to hold her sweet little face between my hands and marvel at her continued existence, but she had already slipped into the backseat with Melody, leaving me standing on the curb.

"Let's go, Mom," Melody called to me, as I stood there, still shaking. "Goosebumps is on next."

But why, I wondered, would some guy she met be talking about a nunnery? Met where? It sounded wrong to me, especially with a name like that. Sisters of Divine Suffering. I talked it over with my husband Ron after dinner that night as we finished off a bottle of Chianti.

You wouldn't think to look at him that Ron had shared my crazy youth with me, that we had met over a tab of LSD. He was no longer bearded, or long-haired, or brown and lanky as he had been in what we now call the sixties, though the excitement started late in that decade and hung on for a while. Balding, just the moustache now, round-tummied, he was still a good-looker, at least to me, but no longer the hippy god I had hooked up with.

He didn't think there was any cause for concern about Carrie. "She's trying something new," he said. "I thought you would like that."

After a certain amount of persuasion, Ron agreed that maybe we should look into it just to put my mind at ease. So he googled the name of the organization Melody had given me, Sisters of Divine Suffering, and after clicking past a few pages of links to porn sites, he brought it up on his screen. It was the most primitive cyberpresence I had ever seen. It made me appreciate how much design went into even the crummiest websites.

There were no ads, not even for prayer books or retreat centers, no banners, no headings, and no links. The only graphic was a line drawing in wavering red strokes that probably represented the convent building, set precariously on a mountainside with a long series of stairs leading up to a tiny door. The text in single-spaced 10-point Comic Sans MS read:

> Sisters of divine suffering is red sisters founded St. Agnes of Siena in the 15th century. Originally from Belgium, now has a single end cloister in the hills north of Santo Domingo Aguascalientes, Mexico. The sisters have vowed remaining silent and give their earthly bonds. They are dedicated to a life of prayer , we are trying to experience the suffering of our Lord on the cross to save share for clean and hello world

The rest of the screen was white. We stared at it together.

"Okay," Ron said. "That's pretty weird. That's not how humans make websites."

"Did you know she was into religion?" I asked, but Ron just shook his head and bugged his eyes out a little. It wasn't just the girls; this whole family seemed to communicate through a system of nonverbal gestures and expressions, which was fine, but I'm not sure I always understand. "Use your words," we used to say to the girls when they were little.

"I hate to think she's buying into the whole Christian thing," Ron said. "Why not something mild like Buddhism? Or just flirt with Transcendental Meditation, like we did?"

I hated to admit it, but I've always had a soft

spot in my heart for the whole Christian story. You can't really get too down on the Baby Jesus and the lambs and all that, for one thing. And I even had a nice feeling about the Easter part of it, God deciding to find out for Himself what all the prayer and lamentation was about by slipping into a people-suit and joining the fray. I imagined the interest He must have felt in all the strange routines and practices and vulnerabilities of the living human body. I especially appreciated that Jesus didn't opt out of the crucifixion, which theoretically He could have. No, He saw the thing through to the end. So that's what they're always complaining about, I imagined God thinking, all the agony and sorrow and betrayal, the flesh assaulted, the hopes dashed, the efforts thwarted, the life ended just as it was getting good.

"How about if you call Melody," I suggested. "Sometimes they tell you things they don't tell me."

Ron pulled out his phone on the spot and had Melody on the other end in no time. And it turned out there wasn't a whole lot more to tell.

"Mexico," he told me. "But we knew that. And her new name is Sister Mary Jesus."

It was no longer a question of if we should go, it was how. Ron had been to Mexico during his dope days, so he was enthusiastic even though he didn't seem to share my sense of urgency. I called Nancy to tell her what was going on and ask her to feed the cat while we were gone. She wasn't as appalled as I thought she would be as a rabid anti-Catholic and devout member of a series of increasingly bizarre Pentacostal churches. She said she always told me I should have taken those girls to Sunday school, but at least it wasn't meth. She had seen a show about meth on TV, and evidently it was rampant. The previous week it had been West Nile virus she was on the lookout for. She agreed to feed the cat and bring in the mail and keep an eye on things until further notice.

After looking at travel websites, maybe locating the convent on the map, though the image was blurry, Ron and I decided to take a train from Juarez and then a taxi to get around Aguascalientes and thereabouts instead of driving. We planned to pay for a Pullman car with a bed, so the train would travel through the night and we would wake up in the heart of Mexico, rested and ready to search for our lost or wayward or beatified daughter.

Of course, it didn't work quite like that. The train was noisy, not in a soothing way, and doors opened and closed, the engine roared and clanked, and we stopped too many times to count, waking each time, checking to see if we were there yet, and trying to sleep again in the few hours that remained. We pulled into our station much too early in the bright, busy morning on market day just as the stands were being set up, leaving the cool dark station and emerging into a scene too confusing for my brain to register.

At first the taxi drivers squabbled over us in high-pitched Spanish, but once things were finally sorted out, we were linked up with Pedro, who assured us that he spoke English very well, *muy bien*, and that he liked "heepees," though how he saw through our respectable veneer is beyond me. He seemed to like us, though, so we didn't try to correct him.

Pedro was to be our guide as well as our driver, and he said he knew all about the sisters of divine suffering and could easily drive us out to their *encierro* whenever we wanted, any time, night or day. We thought we would like to find a good cheap clean hotel first, and it turned out that Pedro's sister Dolores ran the best in town, El Monte, very cheap, very good. He started the car with a wrenching sound and pulled out into the street to the accompaniment of The Rolling Stones doing "Under My Thumb," nosing his way between short dark people with baskets, bags, animals, enormous plates on their heads, and the vendor stands where all manner of smelly ripe goods for sale were stacked as high as the people's heads. The overwhelming impression was of movement, color, and vivid smells of ripe and rotting fruit, shit, and people. Busy, busy, busy, and all I wanted was to sleep.

"Look," Pedro said, pointing ahead, "*la religiosa*, the sister, like you say." Between the golden mangoes of one stand and the bright red meat of the next, almost invisible in the mosaic of color, stood a figure draped in white from head to toe. I strained to see her through the dirty car window, this sister of suffering. Her face was white, like a cave animal, and the stiff cloth around her face was even whiter. She carried a market basket hooked over one arm. As I watched, wondering who she might be in my daughter's new life, she took up five mangoes and offered the vendor some coins. I was surprised to see that he held out a handkerchief for her to place the coins in, turning his face away.

"Why?" I asked Pedro. "Why the cloth for money? Why not just hold out his hand, *el mano*," I said, holding mine out in pantomime.

"Oh those religious," Pedro said, shifting gears and turning around to talk. "Touch the sleeve," he said, pulling at his own shirt to demonstrate, "you are sad all day."

As we threaded our way through the market, I kept noticing how careful the otherwise heedless people were to avoid contact with her even in this jostling crowd, opening to let her pass and then closing in her wake.

"They won't touch her," I said, but Ron hadn't seen it and misunderstood.

"No," he said. "She'll be fine. Carrie's a big girl. Don't worry so much."

El Monte hotel was close by, and though the room was a little spartan, I was too tired to be picky. I wasn't on vacation, after all; I was on a mission to save my daughter. I slept for just an hour or so, and then went out to find Ron and Pedro chattering away in Spanish in the lobby with Dolores in a red muumuu reading a magazine and fanning herself, her black hair floating back and forth in the small breeze she generated. The day promised to be a hot one.

"Now," I said. "I want to go to the place now."

Pedro ushered us back out into the warm street and his brightly decorated taxi, now rocking with Pink Floyd and "The Dark Side of the Moon." Having rested up, I was able to appreciate the dancing of the scarlet fringe glued around the windshield and notice the little picture of Jesus on the dashboard, his big red heart on display outside his robe, his hand raised in admonition.

I thought that if we saw another nun on the way we could offer her a ride. Maybe she would be able to talk if she was off-campus. But that didn't happen. Instead we drove out of the city into the hills, around curving roads, dodging busses that honked, either in greeting or warning, and people returning home from the market. Chickens and goats and pigs crowded onto the road at times, and we had to stop and push our way through them, Pedro honking and talking to us over his shoulder, though I couldn't understand much he said in either Spanish or English.

I just thought about Carrie, and I pictured her ensnared by grim-faced fanatics, beaten and starved, made to suffer for them, trapped in a sweating cell, calling out for help, absorbed into a blank-faced community of zombies. A bug in amber, a fly in a spider web, a leaf in the flood.

Just as I had come to the conclusion that we were hopelessly lost and would never arrive, we stopped and for the first time, I saw the place that held my daughter, up a long flight of steps, just like on the website. It was smaller than it had grown in my imagination, but there was just the door with a barred window in it, the rest of the wall blank and stained. I took Ron's hand and we started up, but Pedro stopped us.

"No mans," he said, shaking his head. "Just for the Mrs."

"Go ahead," Ron said. "Find out what's going on."

It was even more of a climb than it looked like, and each step seemed steeper than the last, so that I was panting when I got to the top, my heart hammering alarmingly in my chest. I knocked.

No one answered, so I knocked again and shouted "Hello?" and then "*Hola?*" and kept up the banging in a way that I hoped would communicate that I was not going to give up. The door opened just a crack.

"Hi," I said. "I'm the mother, *madre*, of one of your group."

"Carrie," I added. Then "Sister Mary Jesus." I hoped it didn't sound as stupid to her as it did to me. "I want to see her. Now."

The crack opened a little wider, and I saw a spectral white figure there, holding her hand outstretched, fingers spread, cocked at the wrist so that I could have given her a high-five.

"What?" I said, "I don't understand," and she pushed her hand out again, so presumably that was all the information she could offer. The door closed.

I turned and looked down the long fall to the taxi where Ron and Pedro were looking up at me. I duplicated the nun's gesture, and saw Pedro nod.

"*Cinco*," he said, when I drew closer. "Come back at five." He held out his watch for me to see. It was three-thirty-five. "*A las cinco de la tarde*," he added.

I couldn't bear the thought of driving away, so Ron agreed we could sit in the cab and wait. Meanwhile, Pedro played the soundtrack of my entire youth on his tape-deck, every song seeming to quiver with hidden messages, dark premonitions, cryptic promises, or threats. I didn't remember the music sounding so sinister, so cruel, but I remembered the phrase "strung-out" we used to use to describe the state I was in, a kind of white-eyed, ragged overload of the senses.

At five exactly, I knocked again and the door opened immediately. I didn't wait for an invitation. I stepped inside.

The room was dark and cool compared to the harsh sun outside, and it took me a while to get my bearings. A little nun stood in front of me, her hands folded peacefully, her habit rustling as she turned and ushered me towards a narrow table, one chair on each side, where I presumed the interview was to take place. I sat heavily, my knees unexpectedly buckling.

"I want to see my daughter," I told the sister, but she had already disappeared down a dim curving hallway. "I want to see her now. At five," I said. "*Cinco.*" And there she was.

Carrie took the chair across from me. Her face was pale, but she had always been very fair, prone to sunburn. I couldn't read her expression at all, and since she sat as still as though cast in stone, there were none of the shrugs or sighs that might have told me anything.

"I am so happy to see you," I said. "How are you, honey? Are they treating you well?"

She remained impassive, immobile, and silent.

I told her I just wanted her to be happy. I said, "If you want out, Carrie, I'll take you home. We can walk out of here today. If they are holding you by force, just wink and I'll come back with as many men or men with guns as it takes to break you out. Just one wink. No one but me can see you. I can get you out of here."

I studied her flat eyes, darker than I remembered in this dark room, waiting for the anticipated wink until my own left eyelid began to twitch. I would do it. I would move heaven and earth, I thought, to save her from this grim silence. "Carrie," I pleaded, "Just tell me."

With what might have been a smile, Sister Mary Jesus reached out across the table with both of her slender hands, a gesture of generosity or a challenge. I thought her hands would be cold, but they were entirely room temperature, like things, as though they had no life, as though they were part of the room. I don't know long we sat like that, hands joined across the table, face-to-face. The contact was so intense and so immediate I didn't have time to think about how I must have looked to her. I was too intent on seeing her, taking in her flat, knowing eyes, her thin cheeks, the faint circles under her young eyes.

As we sat there, I felt a string of pain threading up my arms, growing and stinging, like a transfusion of poison working its way towards my aching heart. I tried to pull away, but Sister Mary Jesus held my hands tight, and I was trapped in the circuit of pain that joined us, that used us both. Tide after tide of anguish jolted me, washing through me, rendering me defenseless on a shore outside of time. This the suffering of the cross, this the unending stream of suffering my daughter had sought, chosen, and embraced. My breath came in short jabs of air, and just as I thought the slicing pain had become intolerable, I felt a quiet singing in my head, a hum of pure pleasure, nothing as soft and expansive as joy, but a sharp, gleeful almost malicious exhilaration, a selfish bliss, and across the table in that cold room, Sister Mary Jesus smiled into my horrified face. Finally she released me, and I ran, leaving my daughter imprisoned there in her ecstatic agony, saving only myself.

I don't remember the ride back to El Monte, only that I cried and I could not stop crying even when the sobs that shook me felt more like vomiting than weeping. I couldn't feel sadness or fear, just the paroxysms that wracked me. Ron held me as well as he could, but clearly he was worried. Pedro just nodded. "Tequila," was all he said. So I spent the evening getting sloshed on tequila, drinking, throwing up, crying, and then drinking some more, as the crying fits gradually became less violent. I stopped around midnight, my belly aching and my head a-buzz. Pedro, who had stayed with us either out of a sense of responsibility, or a fondness for Ron, or possibly for tequila, was still there when I finally fell asleep.

I tried to explain it to Ron the next morning, grateful that he believed me. I tried to compare it to LSD or peyote.

"Like a bad trip?" he suggested.

"The worst and the best," I said.

"Rollercoaster kind of thing?"

"Not even," I said. "The worst and the best all at the same crazy time."

I never tried to explain it to anyone else, but I did go by the apartment to tell Melody it was true, and that Carrie had not wanted to leave the order and come home when given the opportunity. I thought she'd want to know.

"Okay," she said, her eyes drifting toward the flashing television screen, looking over the three heads lined up on the couch, where Kyla, Barry, and Matt, her live-in, sat eating Coco-Puffs almost in unison, mesmerized by the movement of the cartoons, lost in the unreal. She loves her kids, I know, but Kyla's hair was matted and stiff and both of the little ones looked pallid in the half-light. Matt, the latest of a string of guys, unemployed, apathetic, was just a bigger kid she did laundry and bought groceries for, no passion between them that I had ever seen. I looked around the apartment where she lives, my daughter Melody, with nothing beautiful on the walls and nothing an actual human has created anywhere, and I couldn't see anything to love in the stained, standard, synthetic, temporary, caged, regimented, lost world she has accepted, as though she had no choices. I felt a dull aching in my veins where agony had once run, this time a pain that brought no corresponding unearthly delight.

And that's the part of the Jesus story I don't buy any more, the whole savior thing that's supposed to make sense of it. That's the real suffering of Christ, to just hang there on the cross and look around, realizing that you do what you can, but you can't save people from hell. You can't save people from anything.

Little Comfort

Martha sat in the dark, cool space between the bushes and the house, her spine lightly interlocked with the ridges of the overlapping shingles in a way she found particularly comforting. The velvety moss grew thick on the ground there. She had found this hideout only the week before, and she was still enthralled with the soft, green light and the magic of a secret place so close to the house and so unsuspected. Three wonderful diamond buttons lay on a large, flat rock, buttons Martha had stolen the last time she had been sick and her mother had lifted the button box down from the fragrant and mysterious top shelf for her to play Kingdoms with. A small clump of sour clover was turning yellow and limp in the center of the moss where she had stuck it into the mud.

The Princess Delphine stands in the Emerald ballroom in her pink ruffled gown, covered with diamonds, pale golden hair curling down her shoulders. She turns, and Prince Carl is stunned by the depth and sparkle of the fascinating blue eyes she reveals. "Will you dance?" he stammers. The Princess Delphine nods graciously and gracefully places her slender white hand on his shoulder and away they whirl in a haze of perfume and pink mist. Around and around…

"Martha!"

She could see Andrew's grubby black high-tops under the bottoms of the shrubs as he went by, calling her name in his clear, deceptively pleasant voice.

"Suppertime, Martha," he shouted from around the front of the house. She scooched along the wall to where the bay window jutted out, and along the cold cement side of the front porch, and emerged. She was surprised to see how dark it had become and how cool the dusk air was on her hot face. She stood quickly, alert and wary, as Andrew came back around the house.

"Suppertime. Where have you been?" His cool blue eyes surveyed her dirty knees and hands and returned to her tightly guarded face. She was careful not to betray her hiding place with her eyes.

"Does it have a secret, then?" he quavered in his best wicked witch falsetto, forcing her to smile. "You'd better hurry up, Martha. Mom's already mad at you for being late." He gave the advice in that avuncular tone he had assumed ever since his twelfth birthday, when he had begun a series of treacheries, unilaterally dissolving their compact of childhood loyalty and leaving Martha bereft and stunned.

"Come on, Button-face, I'm just trying to warn you. She's really mad."

The first few times Andrew had called her Button-face she had felt obscurely flattered, like a treasured baby sister. Observing her complacent face, he had taken her aside and set her straight.

"Do you know what Button-face means? Boy, are you stupid. It means Butt - on - face, get it? Face like a butt?" He spoke pityingly and with a mock concern that aroused a hate in her heart hot enough to last a lifetime.

"Hello? Martha? Anyone home?"

She gave him a practiced look of scorn and went up the front steps and in to supper, stopping on the way to the dining room to wash her knees and hands. Andrew was probably rushing her so that she would forget to wash and get into trouble. The last time she had fallen for it.

Her father stood behind his chair at the head of the table, a sandy-haired, bushy-eyebrowed fellow, grown soft in the middle, dressed still in his Sunday suit pants with his Sunday white shirtsleeves rolled up to the middle of his beefy curly-haired forearms. With his big padded hands, he pulled out Martha's chair for her, a courtesy playful or perhaps half-mocking.

"A chair for the little lady?" he suggested.

She gave him a gracious smile. *The Princess Delphine*

steps to the throne and sits, settling around her the swirls of her pink satin gown.

"Martha! Since when do you seat yourself before grace? I don't know why a child of mine turned out so unmannerly. Are your hands clean?" She met the accusation in her mother's eyes with a hard, solemn look all her own, and slipped out of the chair. She cast her eyes in appeal to her father.

"Don't talk back, Martha," he said, inclining his face toward her, but avoiding her eyes.

"Andrew? Will you return thanks, dear?"

Andrew folded his hands on the back of his chair, and spoke clearly and evenly. "Dear God, we thank Thee for this day. Bless this food, oh heavenly Father, and the hands that prepared it. Amen."

With a flourish, Andrew pulled out the chair nearest the kitchen for his mother, who sat with a conscious grace, and fluttered her nervous, butterfly hands over the business of napkin, water glass, and silverware.

"Such a headache, I hardly slept a wink last night! Those dogs! Barking and howling till all hours. I don't know what people are thinking of to keep a dog like that! I wouldn't have one around the house." She grimaced with distaste.

"Why do they howl at the train?" Martha asked. "It's like singing or something."

She was momentarily diverted from her mashed potatoes. She loved to lie in bed and listen to the dogs at night, and she counted it as a special boon when she was awake to hear the express train racketing its way through town and the howling of the town dogs when everyone else was asleep.

"I don't know why we can't find a subject for dinner table conversation besides those awful dogs." And her mother began to talk about people Martha didn't know, about the church building committee, so that Martha could no longer keep track or listen, although Andrew cocked his head and looked attentively back and forth between the two adults. Martha sighed and picked up her spoon.

After supper, as Martha stacked the dishes on the counter, Andrew sat at the kitchen table and taunted her.

"Singing dogs, eh Martha? That is one of the stupidest things old Button-face has ever come up with. Are you trying to be stupid, or does it just come natural? My, my." He shook his head in spurious amazement. "I knew you were the ugliest girl in Oklahoma, but I guess you're the stupidest too."

"I am not." Martha was triumphant and sure. "I am not stupider than Janie Frisch, that's for sure. Janie Frisch is a whole lot stupider than me."

Her mother, coming in the door at that moment,

overheard her and her face creased with annoyance.

"Honestly, Martha, I don't know why you can't be more tolerant for those less fortunate than yourself."

"I'm tolerant about Janie Frisch. I just said that she's stupider than me."

"Do not answer back to me, young lady. You will speak when spoken to."

"But you spoke to me, didn't she, Andrew?"

"You are on your way to bed, Martha. Go on. I have just about had enough trouble from you for one day."

The Princess Delphine ascends the stairs, her dainty foot shod in slippers of the palest pink satin. Her hair tonight is as soft as moonlight, and all the people standing below hold their breath as she moves up toward the Throne Room. She looks down at their faces and her heart is filled with a love so sweet and delightful that it causes her to laugh aloud. Her laugh is like a cascade of silvery bells.

Martha stopped on the landing. "Son of a bitch," she said, and waited for a moment or two, her face expectant and serious. Gus Jeffries had told her that morning right after Sunday school that if you said the S. O. B. word out loud that God would strike you dead with lightning. She waited long enough to give Him a chance, and then *the Princess Delphine moves on up the curving stairs in a dark blue velvet cloak as dark as the midnight sky and with diamonds like stars in her hair and on her fingers. She turns at the top of the stairway and looks back at Prince Carl, who adores her. A beautiful smile appears for a brief moment on her petal-pink lips, and he sighs deeply.*

As she quickly brushed her teeth, Martha glanced at her grim reflection in the mirror. "I'm supposed to have Mother's eyes," she thought. But her mother's eyes were appealingly soft and doe-like, not at all like these hard, cynical lumps of mud

Martha ran along to her bedroom, enjoying the soft slip of the flannel as she ran. Sliding her legs between the cold sheets and slapping her head straight back onto the pillow, she forgot to say her prayers and fell asleep with only a quick flash of pink satin.

The dogs woke her up, barking nearby and answering from far away. She could hear the cold night in their voices, the cold night and the cold dirt where they lay on their warm bellies. She wanted to be with them in the wildness and willfulness of their barking, and she pictured herself, Martha the dog, the kind of black dog that has brown eyebrows. She tried a low bark. It sounded like a warning, and she tried again, softly, to bark happily, with the same abandon she was hearing in the yelping of the town dogs.

"Martha, honey, are you okay?" She saw her father's head come through the doorway. She turned on her lamp, and they both blinked and squinted in the glare.

He turned aside for a moment and she thought he was leaving, but he came in and lowered himself heavily onto the side of her bed. His pajama top was buttoned wrong, and she felt a rush of love and longing for him. She sat up and threw her arms around him, nestling her cheek against his rumpled chest.

"Did you have a bad dream, sweetheart?"

"I dreamed that you and Mama died." She was not aware that she was lying.

He rested his bristly face against her satin smooth head and rocked her back and forth. "Oh, well now," he murmured, "Mama and I are not going to die."

"I bet you do," said Martha. She felt him stiffen and his face was hostile as he pushed her away, clonking her head on the hard headboard. His lips twisted and his eyes were hard.

"Daddy's Little Comfort," he said, his voice loud and brittle, and they looked at each other for a long moment. Then he stood and walked out of the room without looking at her again, saying only "Go to sleep, Martha" as he turned off her lamp and opened the door. She saw that he had left a tray outside on the hall table, and as he closed the door, she smelt the unpleasantly mingled odors of chocolate and beef.

She pulled her legs up against her body to capture the remaining warmth of the momentary contact. Sinking her front teeth into one of her rough, dry knees, she let the tears run down her thighs and blot themselves on the soft flannel of her nightgown.

Far away, she could hear the first dog beginning to howl, heralding the arrival of the express train. *The Princess Delphine stands alone at the top of the glacier. All around her the wolves have gathered, and they howl at her as at the moon, cold and lonesome. She looks about her in distress and fear, but Prince Carl is nowhere to be seen. She throws back her golden head, bares her gleaming white throat, and lets the howl that has been buried in her dark soul escape into the frosty, starlit night.* And so softly that she could hardly even hear herself, Martha howled, cold and long, long after the wailing train had raced through town and the dogs were silent and sleeping once again.

Mi Casa

Someone asked me recently if I knew Harve Marshall, and I said, "Oh, sure, I've known him for years. Harve and I are old friends." I was lying. I never liked Harve and I never trusted him, especially when he was most vulnerable. I hated him when he cried. But I'm not a horrible person. He is.

I met him during my favorite summer. I had finally graduated, had been accepted for graduate work at the University of Washington in the fall, and I had three months to spend as I pleased and enough money to tide me over till my fellowship check came. My parents were on their way to Costa Rica, and none of us thought it would be a good idea for me to tag along. Almost all my friends were traveling that summer, but I had seen the South, had smelled and eaten and listened to New Orleans over spring break, and it seemed to me at the time that there was no place l wanted to go. I was tired of talking, of drinking, of smoking. Too many of my friends had taken up with lovers I didn't like. In retrospect, there were a lot of reasons I stayed close to the university, summering in the nearby village of Placita after everyone else had left town. I told myself that I wanted to see what was at the heart of me when everyone else went away. Perhaps it was inertia.

One of the reasons for staying was Mi Casa, a small adobe house which I had known about since my first semester, passed like an heirloom from friend to friend, the house I had fallen heir to because at the last minute someone had decided to go to Europe instead of summer school. I gobbled it up, a house with a name. It had more charm than any place I had lived or have lived since. It fulfilled the country life fantasies of my suburban childhood, it had two fireplaces and a faded red floor, windowsills deep enough to sit in. It was said to be over a hundred years old, not really that old for houses in the Southwest, but older than anyplace I had ever lived.

Since I don't have the knack of creating charm where I live, I appreciate it a great deal when it is handed to me on a platter, with a fig tree and blue gates in the adobe wall around my yard.

I moved in, moved the furniture around a bit, admired the Mexican pottery in the cupboard, and decided which coffee cup I would adopt as mine for the summer, blue and white with a flower and a rooster on it. Moving in was easy, as living there promised to be easy. I like to remember the sun in the kitchen, the long porch where I never did hang a hammock. I have loved particular windows in houses where I have lived since, or shelves, or entryways, and I have certainly lived longer and better in other places. But that was my house for the summer when my time was my own and I had elected to spend it with myself. Even now, many of my dreams set in a city or a theater or nowhere have the private feeling of that little house beside the irrigation ditch, a ditch that ran real water on a timetable I never understood, so it always surprised me like snow.

I believe I had been there only a day or two when I first saw Harve and Nancy unloading groceries out of their van at the house across the road, a little white frame Oklahoma house I thought of as cowboy to my Indian. It had a charm of its own, but it invited domesticity, something I intended to avoid. I thought you might end up canning something if you lived there.

I imagine they came over to visit me as soon as they realized they had a student for a neighbor, but I'm sure it was after I had seen them several times, enough to decide that I liked Nancy. I liked the way she handled a grocery bag, liked the way she walked. She was dark, slender, her hair long and parted down the center like mine, like everyone else's that year. They were my neighbors for that short summer. When they knocked, I let them in. I should have said something cold, something discouraging, but it seemed like too much trouble. And the minute the door closed behind them, they were as erased from my mind as a book I had been lent but was never going to read.

Nancy was so finely turned that I was surprised when I first heard Harve refer jokingly to her awkwardness in a way that made it clear that it was a regular feature in their relationship, counter-balancing, perhaps, his snoring, bad temper, or funny feet. I began to notice afterwards that she dropped things, tripped, spilled hot sauce on her shirt. I enjoyed her prettiness, or rather her charm, in much the same way that I had fallen in love with Mi Casa, my dishes, my life for the summer.

Harve was a grad student in something with lots of words and no feelings—sociology or political science maybe, something that pretends to understand people but doesn't care what happens to them. His long hair and beard and little round John Lennon glasses were standard for the more dedicated college guys. His intellectual conversation bored and embarrassed me, and I tended not to listen. I can't remember what we talked about; it can't have been important. My dislike then was idle and without heat; I was just tired of earnest young men full of ideas and full of themselves.

Our intimacy consisted of coffee some mornings on my porch, or theirs if my hornets seemed in a possessive mood, and once sharing a trip to the grocery store, though I disliked having to hurry up, or wait, or talk about purchases, so I never repeated the experience. I never borrowed books from them. I rarely was alone with Nancy, and she seemed to feel I really had more in common with Harve than with her since I was a graduate student and she was just a wife. She seemed aimless even to me, and yet I remember her walk when she was going down the dusty road alone to check the mailbox as graceful, sturdy, and poignantly female. I was glad she was the one who picked up their mail; Harve would have been neighborly enough to check my mailbox as well, but I suspected he would read return addresses and want to talk about them.

I know it was on the fourth of July when I met Mickey, my summer romance, my dear old cowboy. It undoubtedly helped that I was leaving in two months, and that he would probably live in Placita the rest of his life. So we were experiences for each other to enjoy. Mickey didn't understand me, but his hugs never failed to comfort. I felt I knew exactly how he was put together, but I don't suppose that would have helped in the long run. I had no intention of sharing him with Harve and Nancy, because I was selfish enough to know that he wouldn't have much to say to Harve and would talk to Nancy and I would be stranded listening to the kind of academic chatter I wanted to avoid, knowing I would pick it up again in the fall. I did what I could to keep Mickey to myself. I closed my blue door, I took my phone off the hook, I parked in back.

Mickey and I never talked about life and death and the meaning of it all except when I felt depressed, and then I talked, aware that what I was doing was something I described to myself by that time as "harving." Mickey would listen to me as though I were speaking English backwards or performing some other difficult and unreasonable trick and then would give me his ranch-style hug and say "Come on, honey, I'll take you to the drive-in. That ought to cheer you up." Which made me laugh, which cheered me up, and then we would go to the drive-in.

I saw Mickey most nights and every weekend. Once when Harve came to my door and I felt the dislike welling up in me, I said, "Look, Harve, could you…I mean, uh, this is not really…" and glanced back over my shoulder into the living room where Mickey was settled onto the couch, his lap inviting, ready for love. I almost forgot to return my gaze to Harve, standing on my porch, wrapped in a gummy film of expectation, needy as a ghost, but stickier.

"Sure," he said, "I understand." And he gave my shoulder a squeeze that managed to be brotherly, sneaky and suggestive. I don't know what he understood, but from then on I saw Harve and Nancy occasionally on weekdays and had my time with Mickey unspoiled.

One night around that time, as I lay with Mickey in the old sleigh bed that came with the place, one corner of the frame held up by a number ten can of tomato juice, I dreamed that there was a dry rustling, almost a banging, in the wide space between the screen and the door, something wanting in, and I couldn't tell if the sound that woke me came from my dreaming or my waking. I slid out of Mickey's arms and padded across the wood floor. The sensible thing would have been to open the door to see what was there, but I wanted to know what, if anything, was there before I opened the door. I listened for a long space, but there was only silence.

As I turned away, I glanced at the window on the other side of the room, where the fig tree crowded around the house, and saw two round yellow shapes, like moonlight reflecting in the eyes of a predator, like moonlight on a pair of glasses. Then it was gone and I was afraid to move, afraid I would scream or make that muffled animal grunt that passes for screaming in my dreams. In the end, I crawled back under the covers with Mickey, curving myself around his broad back, and worked my way slowly into a restless sleep.

I tried to tell Mickey about it over breakfast, but he just gave me a hug and a kiss and took off in his truck. I watched him go and it felt different to me than usual, like myself was not enough to do, like I had one foot dangling over a precipice.

After a quick cup of coffee, I walked around back and stepped into the shadow where the fig leaves made a cool shelter against the sun and perfumed the space with the sweet smell of rotting figs, hoping I would remember to wash the sticky juice off of my feet before I tracked it on the floors. There was nothing there to explain what I had seen in the night. Going back into the house, I stopped in the wide space where I had dreamed or heard the scrabbling, but there was nothing there either, just a feeling of unease I brought with me. I tried to pull myself together by deciding I should make curtains to shield myself from the fear of being watched, but in the meantime, as a makeshift, I thumb-tacked a beach towel over that one window. A few days later, the thumb-tacks on one side fell out and the weight of the cloth pulled out the other. I let the whole thing slide down the wall, where it lay against the baseboard until the day I moved out, when my summer was over.

I always loved Mi Casa, but after that night, I began to feel its shelter as a hiding place, or a cage, or a point on the map where I could be found, pinned down. And being anywhere, irrationally, seemed hazardous. My habit of waking frequently during the night, of jerking back to consciousness, or realizing that I have been lying awake in the dark, letting my dream thoughts shift into waking thoughts against my will—that uneasy relationship with the defenseless act of sleep took root and still haunts me at times like the loss of innocence or faith.

In my nighttime waking, standing at one window or another, a cup of cold water in my hand, I thought I saw him from time to time, saw Harve walking down the road to his house, stopping sometimes to gaze upward, but perhaps I was imagining this. I thought I could see him in all the shadows of trees and houses. I know I saw him once sitting motionlessly on the wide accommodating adobe wall that circled my house, but I couldn't tell if he was facing in or out, and I really wanted to know. When he and Nancy dropped by for coffee, I could have asked him about it, but I didn't. I didn't want to know then what he was thinking out there in the dark, and I didn't think he would tell me. I felt even his gaze as pressure. It was irrational; I know that. A reasonable person would have mentioned it, would have said…but I couldn't even start that sentence. And I dreaded the conversation that would follow.

I hunkered down in my house, unwillingly alert, and I mostly quit opening my door when they knocked, instead freezing in place, holding my breath while the adrenalin sloshed around my system, waiting for them to give up. Frustrated, Harve would slap the door, shout my name, and then peer in the window to catch sight of me. I could hear Nancy arguing with him, pulling him away, and in time he gave up. The only contact I had with them after that was when I saw him walking at night, saw Nancy loading or unloading their truck, waved quickly as I slipped into my car to drive to town for a quick beer with Mickey. I was only a little troubled by the occasional sound of raised voices from across the street. At least I knew where he was.

I must have tried hard not to listen because I didn't know how seriously they were fighting until Harve showed up at my door one Sunday morning, much too early, with a grin I don't think he knew was on his face, saying, "I have to talk to you. She's gone, Nancy's gone, she left." I had only answered the door to stop his knocking from waking Mickey up and intended to send him away. But he shoved his way into my kitchen and into a chair, as Mickey came in from the bedroom, rumpled, with bedspread marks on his face. I looked up at him hopefully, as if he might have something for me, but he just stood there, rubbing his neck and waiting to find out what was happening.

"What time is it?" he asked.

"Nancy's gone. She left, I guess." I wasn't entirely awake, and I couldn't remember what to do, if I had ever known.

"You have a fight or something?" Mickey was

looking down at Harve.

"She had no right to run away," Harve said. "And she took the truck."

"What are you going to do? Is there any coffee, honey?"

I realized slowly that the last question was for me, so I gratefully turned my back on the situation and began the morning coffee ritual. Empty the pot, wash the pot, fill the pot, put in the coffee, put on the lid, plug it in, and no one was saying anything, so I knew it was going to be my baby. I turned back and looked at Harve, who was waiting for me with that shit-eating grin on his face.

"What are you going to do?" I asked.

"I think she took the money out of the bank. You realize," he said suddenly enraged, "that means she's been planning this for days. Why the hell didn't she tell me? She didn't give me a chance to do anything."

"What are you going to do?" I asked again. I imagined spending the rest of the day asking Harve what he was going to do, but this time I sat down at the table across from him and put my elbows on the table in a planning sort of way.

"Do?" said Harve. "What am I supposed to do when she runs off without even trying to let me know what's going on with her? No," he said, "she just dumps everything on me and splits. Jesus Christ!"

I didn't think I could ask again, so I was relieved when Mickey sat down with us. I felt sick, I hated Harve for being in my kitchen, and I wanted everything to happen backwards until I was nested with Mickey in bed, just barely conscious, whole.

"Where do you think she went?"

"She could be anywhere." Harve wasn't looking either of us in the face. It seemed to me that I was the one who was shaky, lost, jarred and bereft, who had to decide what to do.

"How much money?"

"Five hundred dollars."

I was so irrationally relieved to get a definite answer, I had to stifle the impulse to get a pencil and paper and write it down. $500.00.

"Maybe she'll be back." Mickey was trying to comfort Harve, who just looked stubborn. "Maybe she'll think better of it," he said soothingly.

"No." Harve was adamant. "She just takes a relationship and walks out. Well, I don't need her. I don't need someone who sneaks around behind my back like a goddamn sneak."

I could tell that Mickey was sure that the sneaking had included another man, that Nancy had run off with someone, but I was sure he was wrong. I was sure that Nancy was alone somewhere on the road; I could picture her so clearly, one arm flat on the steering wheel, her elbow resting in the open window, heading for someplace, her hair flapping in the wind, humming a little, afraid but pleased with herself, by herself, alone. I would so much have preferred to be sitting next to her rather than locked in with Harve and Mickey.

"Listen, Harve, I'm really sorry this had to happen. Maybe you'd better call her parents, they might know something, or maybe a friend or somebody. There must be someone you can think of that she'll be in touch with."

"Yeah, I guess I have to."

I was watching Harve closely like a physician trying to diagnose a particularly tricky case when Mickey got up, put on his hat, kissed me, and walked out the door in one motion, saying to Harve, "Good luck" and to me, "See you later, sugar."

He didn't like Harve much either, and it was my kitchen, not his. As the door closed, Harve began to cry, making a huffy noise, and then a series of high whimpers. I didn't want to, but I reached across the table and touched his arm, patted his shoulder and said, "Hey, take it easy, it's okay," until he raised his head and looked at me angrily.

"You think it's my fault," he said, glaring. "You think I deserve to be shit on."

"Take it easy, " I said, "just take it easy. You've had a heavy kind of shock, so just take it easy."

I made us both some breakfast while Harve told me over and over that she was gone, that she had planned it, that he didn't know what to do, and every time he repeated it I felt better about it, more like something lucky had happened. After the last piece of toast was gone, the last of the coffee poured out into our cups, I looked up and there was Harve, still looking at me expectantly.

"Listen, Harve, it's nine-thirty, why don't you go on home and call up her folks and see if they've heard from her. They might have heard from her. Go on…"

"They'll think I was mean to her. They'll think I wasn't good enough for her."

"No," I said, "they'll be concerned. They'll be sorry if things are going wrong. I'm sure they won't blame you."

I wasn't sure at all. How could I have been? But I wanted Harve to leave. I wanted to feel the magic house close around me like it had when I first moved in, no words, no tricks, just a house, just a day, just what I needed. When he left, I could tell he felt cheated. I hadn't given him what he felt he deserved, because he thought we were friends. Letting Harve believe his own lies was cruel. That's why I gave him anything at all, because I felt guilty. I felt in a perverse way that I owed him whatever I could scrape together.

He came back much sooner than I expected and

said, "They weren't home," and my heart sank. I felt a moment of panic, but then I excused myself, told him to keep trying, and took off for the Chinese Star Lounge where I found Mickey, as I knew I would. We had a few beers, played the jukebox, played a little pool, which I never liked and was hopelessly bad at. I would probably have done almost anything to keep from going home. I went to Penney's and looked at clothes, but I didn't have any money to spend. I spent the rest of the day back at the Chinese Star, playing the jukebox some more, mostly choosing songs I'd never heard before. We didn't talk about Harve or Nancy. I was very glad when I saw that Mickey was going home with me.

Harve was back as soon as I stepped onto my porch. Mickey made up a fire in the round adobe fireplace, just to look at, and then sat and watched us, tolerant, not really listening. I'm sure he believed we were friends because we had given every appearance of being so, and I was embarrassed to admit we were really combatants. Harve just kept talking and challenging me to say the right thing back, which I never could do. It was like trying to help someone who hates hats buy a hat. We played it almost like a game: he would play guilt, I would counter with fate, he would maneuver over into sorrow, I would extend comfort, he would refuse, I would offer philosophy, he would erupt into anger. It went on late into the night, and I couldn't leave, because it was my house. And I couldn't say what he wanted to hear, that Nancy was bad and he was good, and I didn't say what I wanted to hear either.

I was jumpy all the next day. I swept the faded red floor, but couldn't find the dust pan, so I left a little pile of crumbs, dust, ashes, spider webs, whatever falls off and settles in a kitchen, and by the end of the day, much of it was redistributed over the floor, and I found the dust pan under the bed. That's the kind of day it was. The walls seemed to be closer together, the windows smaller, and the air thicker than I remembered. I felt like a frog in a box.

Harve showed up after supper, and he began again, telling me the history of his relationship with Nancy, how they met, how they got serious, married, their sexual problems, her defensiveness, his own irritability. He talked a great deal more the second night, and I talked less. I was waiting for him to go away, and yet I am sure I said many fitting and perceptive things to him. But I never said, "We all love you, Harve. You are good." I could see that Mickey was bored with the words that filled the air like feathers or smoke, something you want to brush away but can't.

Mickey didn't come to see me the next night, which I felt as desertion although I couldn't really blame him. The whole thing bored him. He probably thought

Harve should just go get drunk, as he might have done. I missed looking at him while Harve talked, missed the goldy-red hair on his forearms, his nice big hands, his neat little ears, and the way his thighs curved down to the knee. He always looked so good to me.

Harve came over to be fed dinner and stayed till 1:30 the next morning. It felt like everything I said to move him along sucked me deeper into the muck. In the end, I sat and said nothing, bludgeoned into silence by his relentless words. He had begun to take on both parts in the conversation. He wrinkled his forehead and spoke as though he were reading, trying to pretend he was speaking. He spoke like a very bad actor reading his lines for the second or third time.

"What really gets to me is that she didn't really ever try to talk it out. She always said she wasn't any good at talking, but it seemed like she could talk to other people. I guess it's partly my fault, though. I mean, I'm sure I didn't make things any easier for her. I really tried to be patient, but I guess I wasn't very good to her. She was so neat. I really cared about her. I'm so sorry now for all the times I was mean. I guess life is just like that. Maybe she'll be better off. Maybe I'll be better off. I guess we had just learned everything there was to learn from each other. I hope she's happy. I just wish she had told me, that we could have talked about it instead of running off like that. I had to borrow some money from my folks. It just really seems crazy not to tell me, to take the money out of the bank and never tell me. It really pisses me off that she didn't have enough courage or respect to at least…"

In my childhood, I had read lots of fairy tales, in which wishes, challenges, and ogres come in threes. This must have contributed to my surprise and chagrin when Harve came around the fourth night. I felt a really savage surge of irritation, but I let him into the sitting room where I had been enjoying Mickey's story about a plumber his sister's next-door neighbor had married who was a little deaf. I never did hear the end of that story. That fourth night, Harve talked about Nancy in a spuriously analytical way, about her paranoia, her clumsiness, her skinny ass, her frigidity, ugliness, stupidity, craziness, telling me about the time she freaked out at a party given by the head of Harve's department and hid under the porch with the family dog. He talked like an ugly thing that can't stop happening, with malice, with spite, and he looked at me out of the side of his face to see how I would react. Mickey yawned, and Harve stood up and stretched as if he had just finished a big meal and was satisfied.

I realized how tight I was, my muscles like snakes constricting my bones, my head throbbing with weariness. As I walked Harve to the door, my knees trembled and I kept my hand on the wall. Outside the screen door, Harve turned and said, "I guess I just can't get it that I don't have to feel guilty."

As I closed the door, instead of good night, I said, very quietly,"I hate you, Harve." I turned away without waiting to see if he had heard me and began to cry like a child, not like the grown-up person I wanted to be. If my mother had been there, I would have crawled into her lap. Mickey held me and comforted me, let me cry, stroking my neck and arms as if I were a baby animal or someone dying. "He's just crazy, sweetie. Never you mind about him, he's just crazy and upset."

"No," I said, although I was breathing ragged and finding it almost impossible to talk. "No, he's so awful he makes me hate everything. And I can't do anything, I just get paralyzed and guilty and sneaky-feeling, like I'm lying. And I am lying, I'm lying worse than he is. He's so empty, so creepy and awful. It's not what he does, it's what he is. Don't you even feel it? Don't you understand?"

Good old Mickey held me away from him and said again, gently and carefully so I would listen, "I think probably he's just crazy. He talks like probably he is."

I moved back into the circle of his arms, shook my head "no" against his chest and we sat there with our arms around each other, and I rested.

The next morning I found a note from Harve on my door, saying he had gone to Denver to visit his folks and think things over. I had a week left before I had to leave for Seattle, and every day of that week as I packed up, I was looking over my shoulder, afraid that he would reappear, wanting, demanding, requiring, and I would have nothing left to defend myself with.

I had read none of the books I had brought with me. I had done no sewing, no gardening, no writing. I didn't even have a tan. But as long as I was able to end my summer with a fond good-by to my house and to Mickey and not to see Harve, I was satisfied. I knew Mickey wouldn't write to me so I didn't even try to keep in touch. But every time I have found myself in love it has been with a man who has some of the same maternal touch. And every time I have broken off with someone, I have imagined running to Mickey. He drove over to see me off, giving me a big hug and a kiss, saying, "You take care of yourself, honey. There's a lot of love riding with you."

I said, "Oh, Mickey," helplessly and climbed into my packed car. I took his picture as I pulled out, of Mickey still watching me, standing in front of my house, the house not mine any more, the house of my dreams.

When I first came here to teach, I saw Harve's name in the college newsletter with dismay. I felt a quick impulse to back out of my new appointment, the result of years of scrambling effort. But that's a child's reaction. This is a big institution; he's in a different department. My name is unremarkable enough that he might not even make the connection if he saw it somewhere. And I was no longer the wide-open girl of that summer. I worried more about getting my office set up, painted the right shade of white, the doorframe bright blue, my framed photographs centered on the wall where the sun would light them up: a formal portrait of my parents, my three nieces with their new puppy, flowers backlit by a Tuscan sunset, Mickey looking like a Hollywood extra in front of Mi Casa.

Harve did, in fact, find me. I looked up from working at my desk several weeks into the semester to see him standing in the doorway of my office with his arms held wide for an old-friends, long-time-no-see hug, on his face the look I remembered—a mix of greed and shame, shamelessness and hangdog defiance that used to make me cringe. I rose and walked towards him, shaking my head, saying, "No, oh no, no, no, not at all, no way," not in fear, but with a spontaneous desire to correct what was wrong and blot him out entirely. There must have been something in my face or my voice, because he dropped his arms and stepped back as if from an unexpected oncoming train.

"Oh no," I said again, "this is just not happening,"

and I closed the door firmly in his face. And that was the end, because I knew in a way I can't explain that my life was no longer, perhaps had never been, a stream in which I could float passively, letting events flow over and around me, but a river I would have to depend on myself to navigate using all the skill and craft I could command, fair weather or foul, hell or high water. I went back to the paper I had been grading before I was interrupted and read on, looking for the meaning at the heart of it.

Mercy

There must have been thousands standing in the rain that day. Duke says hundreds, but I had the better view. I could see people fanned out on both sides and across the road where Duke had parked the Christamobile, ready to hopefully sell-out our Christa memorabilia once the funeral was over. I calculated that if each one of those believers bought an average of just one prayer poster or healing candle at an average of $10 each, we'd have more than enough to call it good and move on. Since this was their last chance, the take could be a lot more than that, I figured. We'd just have to wait and see.

I knew Duke was thinking we could stretch the gig out another month or so just on the memory of Christa, but I could see the handwriting on the wall, and it said to get while the gettin's good, so that's what we were going to do. Social Work had started sniffing around again, and there was going to be more explaining than I felt up to. It was time to close up shop.

You could see these were not high-class people

getting wet out there by the number that didn't even have umbrellas, just standing there like chickens in the poultry yard, gawking and sniffling. Or their umbrellas were a bright color not really fitting for an occasion such as the laying to rest of a true prophet—or whatever she was—like Christa. I didn't intend to take any chances on catching pneumonia like she had, so I was sheltered under a faded black umbrella with a carving of a naked woman on the handle Duke had brought me from the Philippines when he was still a Merchant Marine. When I first got it, her tits were painted cherry red, but time had worn them down to plain wood, and I was holding my hand over that part anyway.

I ran over my speech in my head, knowing that there was no way I could memorize anything that long and I would have to act like I was just saying it, sneaking little peeks at the paper once in a while. Duke's English teacher at the college had already had a look at it, so I figured it was good that way, all cleaned up and ready to go. My turn came after the preacher did the ceremony with all the usual church stuff. It was my first and last speech on the subject of Christa, since I had tended to stay in the background, being safer that way, and I intended for it to pack a wallop, so I gave it at full volume.

"My friends," I started out. "My friends, my

brothers and sisters in the Holy covenant. We lost Christa last week and this week we are laying her in this hollow ground." Hallow, according to the teacher. "This hallow ground," which I had changed back to "hollow," like in the Lord's Prayer. I paused at this point to let the sadness kind of soak in, because some of them were sure to cry out at that and that would make the others break down as well. I wanted to give them some time to turn to each other for consolation and build up the mood.

"But she is not really gone, my friends, is she? We have her here," and just like I planned, I started in clutching at my heart at this point, "here in our hearts and souls. She has touched each one of us with her special gift of God's love, each in the way we were most needful, for she saw our need and gave unstintingly of herself." Unstintingly was another teacher word, but I left it in because I liked the sound of it. Unstintingly.

When we first found her, Duke and me, we had no idea how she was going to pay off. I just couldn't see it at first when we didn't hardly even know what she was supposed to be. She was just a little screetchy naked thing chained down in the basement of Duke's late uncle Jessup's house. We undid her and got her upstairs, gave her some soup out of a can and cleaned her up as best we could. We clothed her in some of Jessup's old long johns, rolling up the legs and sleeves till there were big doughnuts around her little ankles and wrists. We had no idea she was even down there, but Jessup had died the week before, so she was more than half-starved. I guessed she was maybe ten years old, but Duke said no, to take a look at her titties, she was a woman grown. And I told him to keep his eyes to himself, but he was about right. No taller than up to my elbow and jumpier than a frog. Every time I looked at her, she raised up her hands and sort of pushed them at me, like a preacher calling down the Holy Spirit. Or she would press her hands together like she was starting to pray. There was something about her that made you a little uneasy at first.

I was in favor of dropping her off at the Social Work and letting them take the trouble, but Duke, who is smarter than he looks, said no. Nobody knows about her, and that means we should just take our time and see what we got here. We just called her Baby at first. Christa was after we got into the faith-healing business. It turned out she couldn't anymore talk than a dog, just babbling sometimes. Later on we would use that, call it speaking in tongues. But that night Duke set her down at the kitchen table and gave her some word lessons, like he had heard some guy talking about teaching a parrot.

"Now I lay me down to sleep," he said, holding her by the cheeks so she'd pay attention, squeezing if she started to wander off. "Now I lay me down to sleep," over and over till she finally started to say something like that back to him.

"Now I weep," she said.

Duke looked over his shoulder at me, where I was leaning on the counter having a smoke. "Did you ever meet my uncle Harley?" he asked.

I hadn't so I didn't say anything back.

"He had a mule who could count up to seven and do adding and subtracting. He made a mount of money off that mule." Duke grinned. "I think we might have a mule here we can use."

He turned back to her and said, "Jesus loves you," and she said "Now I weep," and he squeezed her face hard and gave her a little shake so she'd concentrate and change tracks. "Jesus loves you," he said, and she said it back to him right away like a good little record player. "Jesus loves you," she said, looking him straight in the eye, and there was something touching about her way of saying it, like it might be true.

After a few more weeks, hanging out at Jessup's place, working out our plan and getting Christa trained, we were ready to take her on the road, just to see what we had and how it would go. We took Jessup's old truck to town and traded it in for a sandwich truck with the side flaps that come up to serve customers. Duke painted it sky blue and tried to put some angels on there, but they came out too sexy so he had to paint them over. That's when we decided to call her Christa. He painted "Christa" in white letters outlined in black, and it looked pretty smart. He added a cross in each corner, with lines behind it like it was rushing along heading for Christa's name.

We set up outside the most Holy Roller church we could find a few towns over, but on a side street by the parking lot, not out in front. We had her dressed in a sparkly gold choir robe from the Goodwill, and set her up on the sidewalk on a bar stool draped in baby blue, looking like a little angel herself. Her hair had finally got untangled after a number of shampoos and creme rinses, and curled all blonde and shiny. We told her to bless people like Duke had been teaching her.

"Bless you, my friend," she would say. "Jesus loves you." I had thought she should say "bless you, sister" or "bless you brother," but she couldn't be counted on to use the right one with the right person. The feeble little thing had no idea what she was saying. But she did peer at each person with a truly loving look, as though each one of those ugly faces was a miracle to see, which to her it might have been if all she had seen was Jessup up to that point. And once she had blessed someone, they might slow down and watch to see her bless the next one.

The turning point came when one old woman held

out her hand to Christa in fellowship, and Christa just grabbed and held on to her, saying over and over that Jesus loved her, and the old woman started hopping around a little, saying her pain was gone, the neuralgia the doctors couldn't cure had actually left her body and she was made whole in the love of Jesus. That really got a crowd gathered up, and most people had some kind of complaint to get cured of. Duke quickly positioned a collection basket on a little table next to Christa, just in case they had something left to give after being fleeced by the preacher inside. Christa clung onto each one like holy Moses, and Duke had to pry them apart.

"You're healed," he would yell out as he flung them off, and it was just like on TV.

"I'm healed," they would shout, and more would come around. We had thought I would have to pretend to have something wrong with me get healed, though I'm healthy as a good horse, but it turned out we got along fine without that. Christa was healing the sick left and right and blessing everybody and you could see she was enjoying herself, too.

Things kept on going like that until the preacher appeared in the church doorway, looking over at us with a non-Christian expression on his face when he saw what we were up to, and we took off, promising the crowd that we would come again to continue the ministry, this time to the next town, after Christa had recuperated from the divine energy that had run through her body, giving herself to the Lord's work. We counted the take when we got back to Jessup's, and it was close to three hundred dollars. We were in business.

"Christa loved you all," I said to the multitude gathered there for that last time, "just as your Father in Heaven loves you, sending his only begotten Son Jesus Christ to save you from a life of sin and damnation. His daughter Christa—" and here I was skating a little close to the line of being a blasphemer. We always tried to keep the exact nature of Christa's ties to God kind of hazy and open to interpretation. "His daughter Christa has departed this life, but she is now enjoying a new life with her Father in Heaven, who has called her back home." I stopped here to get some amens and a few hallalujahs, and I was not disappointed. It looked like someone towards the back of the crowd had fainted, which was all to the good.

"She has given us everything"—a little nudge here on the pocketbook, I hoped—"and paid the ultimate price for the work she has done for us, God's work. Let us thank her! Let us thank God!"

There was lot more like that written down for me, and after I said it all, I turned the show back over to the preacher for a final prayer and hotfooted it over two blocks to bring in the truck we had rented with the last of the Christa stuff in it to restock the Christamobile as needed. Over a thousand people there to bury her, and some of them not even close enough to hear a word, so they would be willing, I thought, to stand in line and wait their turn in the rain, which was letting up a little, to purchase these sacred and collectible items. We always tried to emphasize both of those points in our pitch.

We had done our best to take good care of Christa, within limits. We couldn't have her getting all fat and sassy—it would have ruined the effect of this skinny, ghostly, pale figure reporting, as near as you could tell, directly from the mouth of God himself. A fat little woman just couldn't do that unless she had a lot more mother wit than Christa seemed to possess.

Early on, the Social Work got interested in having her evaluated, once they had got wind of her being in our custody, as they put it. They wanted to see what she had to say for herself, which was a laugh. Duke spent three days telling Christa over and over not to open her mouth at all, that they would cut out her tongue if she did. I don't know if she understood it, but he scared her enough with his knife that she didn't say a peep in that office where I had to take her, even though I had better things to do with my time than sit and look at magazines with a bunch of low-downs.

Duke did all the teaching part, and Christa kept her

eyes on him all the time, looking to see what he might want her to do. I even thought towards the end of her time with us she was starting to understand some of our talk. When we said we were fixing to leave, she'd go stand by the door like a good hound dog does, and she learned to beg for food at the supper table. Duke taught her to call food "mercy," so that if she started going on about it during one of the shows, it would fit right in. "Mercy," she might say, and whatever fool it was would praise God and put some more money in the plate.

How she died was a pity. We knew she was a little poorly when we could hear her down on her little cot coughing away, but Duke got aggravated and yelled at her to shut up or he would come down and shut her up. She knew full well he meant it when he got riled up like that. So that's how she got the pneumonia started, I guess, and a week or two later her fever shot up, and her babbling about God and Jesus and mercy—it was a scene like I don't want to see ever again. Her eyes stared up out of her head like a wild thing, and when she grabbed at me to keep me from shutting off the lamp, her hands burned me like hellfire. I shook her off, but I told Duke in bed that night that we needed to find her some aspirin somewhere. And he agreed, so we fully intended to take care of her, like we always did. We couldn't afford not to, the kind of money she was bringing in.

But the next morning she was gone, leaving behind that scrappy little frame with nothing in it, almost hidden in the horse blanket we had provided for her. I like to broke down and cried.

"She's gone," I called up to Duke, and he came thundering down the stairs, thinking she had run off somewhere. "She's met her Maker," I said. And I have to admit, I felt kind of sad, like I would miss her, miss being told Jesus loved me every time I turned around, miss getting to add to the cushion of dirty bills, dollars, fives, tens, sometimes twenties, we were building up in a trunk at the foot of the bed.

We took off to Florida as soon as we could get shut of the funeral and the after-funeral sale, which was even more than I had calculated, on the highway in a new truck well before dark came on. Social Work can do what it wants for all I care, it's not going to bring her back. It can dig her up but just like always, she won't have a word to say for herself. And we're clean across the country minding our own business, so it's nothing to do with anybody else.

Of course, it's not the same without her, just the two of us again. Duke had to go and find some Florida school where he can waste his time, doing homework at his age. He says there's always something new to learn. I guess he's right enough. I didn't imagine when we first got Christa how it was going to go, but I learned something from having her. I once was blind, as the song goes. I once was blind, but now I can see. Now I can see opportunities I was blind to before. I don't intend going to school like Duke, but I been looking around lately for something to do—maybe a little light nursing of the elderly or looking after rich people's babies.

Mates

"I think you may be thinking of lemurs," he says. "Is that possible?"

"Lemurs," she repeats thoughtfully. "Okay, I guess I was. Lemurs are primates; shrews are what... rodents?" She has already abandoned the conversation, her hands and eyes occupied with sorting and stacking the papers and books on her desk. Bills. She wants to buy a black silk jacket. She can picture it. The phrase "sell-out" floats idly through her brain but she can't think of a market off-hand.

"Although," he says, "I understand that primates are supposed to have evolved from squirrel-like, tree-dwelling rodents. I like that. It makes me feel more at home with my species."

The apartment is still except for the sound of the traffic outside and the murmur of the life support systems of refrigeration and temperature control. Two computers hum side by side on the long brown table they use as a desk. One screen saver tells the time in big white numbers; the other shifts from rain to fish to stars at thirty-second intervals.

"Leandra is coming over at 3:00 after her class." She plants herself on the couch and watches him.

"I know," he says. "It's Friday."

"I wish you liked her better. She's going through a very hard time. Why don't you like her?"

"I could try to analyze it for you," he says, "but it would just take time. It wouldn't change anything."

He turns and walks into the kitchen, out of her sight, and she can hear the clink of the jar of coffee beans and the sound of the grinder being set on the counter. He makes coffee whenever he feels like it, not in the morning after a shower. He showers whenever he feels like it—twice a week or twice a day; it doesn't seem to matter. She needs a schedule that says: Sleep Now, Drink Coffee Now. He's a miracle man, familiar as a cousin and unpredictable as fate.

"Are you going to work?" she calls into the kitchen.

"Of course I'm going to work. I always work."

"I mean, are you going to the office today?"

"Maybe. Why?"

"I just wondered." She wants him elsewhere when Leandra comes. She is always aware he's in the house by the fresh-baked smell of him, even in the bedroom with the door closed. She wants to fit into her own skin again, whole and round as an unbitten apple, tight-skinned and shiny.

"She whines." His dark, curly head protrudes out into the hall as he peers at her.

"She whines?" Her voice rises incredulously. "My God, her husband just died—she's got a right to whine!"

He shrugs. "I know. That's why I don't like her though."

"If you were to die…" Something in his sad monkey eyes stops her. "Okay, I know, everybody dies. When you die," she corrects herself, "if you die before I do, I'm going fall into a million pieces and scream at God and be a problem to everyone I know. I'd be a lot worse than Leandra."

"But you won't whine," he says. "I don't like her voice is what it is."

He comes around and sits next to her on the couch, squeezing her knees affectionately with his wiry paws, then leaning down and kissing them lingeringly, one after the other.

"I like you," he says, smiling at her.

"Why can't you like my friend?" she says. "I like your friends."

"That's good," he says, untying one of her shoes, twisting down awkwardly from where he sits. "I like your sister." He takes off her shoe and begins to explore up her pants leg to find the top of her sock.

Just as he succeeds in pulling her sock off, the phone rings and he answers it, "Y'ello," standing by the desk, toying with the phone cord as he listens.

"Which version?" he asks. He hangs up and begins to gather papers and files from the desk and shove them into his briefcase, so she knows he is going to the office.

He plants a kiss on the top of her head and closes the door behind him, leaving her sitting alone with a shoe in her lap and a sock draped over the arm of the couch.

She doesn't move for a long time. Then she stretches and stands up. Her computer screen says 2:14 PM. Between thoughts, she pads to the desk with the sensations in one bare foot and one shoe foot dividing her down the middle.

Therapy

I walked into her office, my legs stiff and my chest tight with apprehension. She closed the door behind me as I sat down. There was the usual box of Kleenex on the table next to the chair. She sat down across from me and we looked at each other. She was blonde with very fine features, her nose thin and slightly hooked and her eyes a pale gray-green. She was small, her vanilla-colored clothes seeming professional and expensive. So clean and smooth. When she smiled, her teeth were as small and pointy as a three-year-old's.

"What can I do for you, Ellie?"

"I don't know," I said.

"What are you here for?" she asked.

"I'm here for impotence," I said. I had decided that was what I would say before I left the house. I felt relieved to have said it.

"Sexual impotence?" she asked.

"No, I don't think so." I said. "Just impotence."

"Tell me about it."

I was studying her, hoping to see a twinkle or a

warm patch where I could connect and feel a little safer. But I wasn't at all sure that feeling safe was a good thing or if it was actually part of the problem.

"I do a lot of things, creative kinds of things, but it doesn't go anywhere. It doesn't get out. I just do it."

"What kinds of things are we talking about here?" She was looking at her folded hands, a small silver ring on her little finger. Such small hands. She looked up and caught me looking at her hands. "Well? What are the creative things that you do?"

"I write satires, and poems, and I write songs and sing. And I design clothes and I paint a little. And I write plays sometimes. And sometimes I make greeting cards for people. Stuff like that."

She sat in silence and studied me. I watched her, and the silence grew and spread like dark molasses in the room. I was beginning to get comfortable, when she asked me, "And you feel impotent?"

"Yes."

We sat in silence again. I felt a sudden wild desire to put my head in her lap and let my tears out. I could feel the tears beginning. I am so tired of crying. I can always cry. I started crying, and I felt her move closer. She smelled expensive. I buried my head in my hands, snuffling. She put a Kleenex into one of my hands. After I blew my nose, she put her hands on my knee.

"I can help you," she said. "Our time is almost up.

Let's make another appointment for next week."

As I left, she said, "It's nice to know you, Ellie."

"You look sad today."

"No, I'm just tired. Darby woke up at 3:00, and when I went in, I couldn't find Tanky for him for the longest time."

"Who's Tanky?"

"His tank. He sleeps with his tank."

"Your two-year-old sleeps with a tank? How do you feel about having a child who sleeps with a military device like that?"

"Darby's okay."

"How can you allow your child to sleep with a tank? Why does he need that kind of protection? Is he a fearful child?"

"No, he's okay. I don't understand about Tanky. I've been waiting till Darby can talk to ask him about it."

"Just close your eyes now, Ellie, and imagine that you are Darby. Tell me about Tanky, Darby."

I could picture Darby's round, rosy face and round eyes. "I want Tanky," I said.

"And why do you want Tanky?"

"Tanky loves me."

"Doesn't mommy love you, Darby?"

"Wait a minute," I said, opening one eye. "Mommy

loves Darby just fine, and Darby knows it."

"This seems to be making you angry. Can you get in touch with that anger?"

"I don't see why it matters who Darby loves. For some reason he loves Tanky. That doesn't mean that I don't love him." I was pleading with her.

"But Ellie, what kind of mother gives her child a tank to love?"

"I didn't give him Tanky. He found him."

"You're going to have to face it, Ellie. This kind of behavior can be one sign of a very disturbed child. Your child is in trouble and you're in denial about it."

I could feel a familiar misery trembling in my gut. My hands were cold again. The office was very cold. I began to cry.

"That's all we have time for today. Your homework for this week is to look at your child. Just watch what he does. There are certainly other signs to look for. Tantrums. Extreme isolation. Talk this over with your partner if you wish." She patted my shoulder. "See you next week."

When I got home, Frank and Darby were on the couch playing a card game Darby had invented called "Put." It consisted of putting the cards in stacks according to some principle I couldn't grasp, but Frank did sometimes. He tried once to explain it to me. He said it had to do with taking turns, but you have to take turns taking turns. I didn't get it. They seemed so warm and unconscious, and the idea of my Darby being in trouble hit me in the gut. I burst into tears, and my backpack slid off my shoulder and onto the floor.

"Mommy hurt?"

"No, Darby, I think she's just upset." Frank sounded kind but so far away.

I reached down for Darby, but he struggled out of my arms and ran from the room. What kind of child doesn't want to be held by his mom? What kind of child runs away when his mother cries? I collapsed the rest of the way onto the floor, sobbing. Then I smelled the strange mix of lovely smells and dirt that is Darby, and I felt cold, sticky plastic against my cheek.

"Tanky makes it better, Mom. Okay?"

"Tell me about yourself, Ellie. It sounds like you're a highly gifted and creative woman."

"I guess. Not that it does a lot of good. It's just something I do like other people do the things they do. It's just what Frank calls primate shit."

"And how do you feel about your lover calling your creative work shit? Does that bother you?"

"No," I tried to explain. "It's like the thing where elephant shit is when you get pompous and chicken shit is getting trivial. So primate shit is not being able to leave things alone, having to re-design everything. Making great art or making toilet paper covers out of Clorox bottles. Just making things or making things different. Like chimps do. That's all it means."

"So it doesn't bother you to have what you do described as shit."

"People call all kinds of things shit. It's like slang."

"Tell me about Frank."

"Oh," I said. "Well, he's kind of hard to describe. I mean, physically, he's very easy to describe. But, I don't know, he's kind of a weird guy."

"What is it in you, Ellie, that makes you choose a weird guy to relate to? Why would you choose to be with a weird guy?"

I thought for a minute. "The normal guys are too weird."

Her eyebrows went up. "Are you making a joke?"

"Not really," I said. "It just seems like that."

"So, you said Frank is easy to describe physically. Why don't we start there?"

"You know the Citadel Bookstore?"

"Yes," she said.

"Frank is the guy who owns it." I was used to Frank by this time, but I've never got used to the way people react to him.

Her eyes widened. I thought they might. "Not the really short little guy with the suit and tie?"

"Yup," I said. "That's Frank. Francis Xavier Goldbloom."

She studied me for a minute. "You are not a small woman, Ellie."

"I know," I said sadly. I am not a small woman.

"And yet you choose to be with a man who must be a foot shorter than you."

"Seven inches, actually. I'm 5' 7", he's 5 feet."

"What is that like for you?"

"Sometimes it's a little weird. But when we have our heads on the pillow we're the same height. It works pretty well. I'm really attached to Frank. He's a very sweet person."

"Why do you want a man who's so much smaller than you? What does that say about the power structure of your relationship?"

"I don't think I would necessarily have chosen a short guy, you know, if it wasn't Frank. Although I might now. I don't know what the power structure of our relationship is like. He's very sweet. He really is." I could picture him, the endearing combination of small and masculine that he is. Dark silky hair on his body. Pale chalky skin. Sharply defined muscles in miniature on his arms and legs. "What a doll," I sometimes thought.

"Are you a lesbian, Ellie?"

"No," I said. "I don't think so."

"But you're not sure."

"I'm hardly ever sure," I said. "I'm perpetually ambivalent. It's one of my problems."

"Why do you think you have chosen to be with a man you can dominate physically?"

"I can't," I said. "He's little, but he's still stronger than I am if that's what you mean."

"Doesn't being with him make you feel big and strong?"

"Well," I said. "I don't know. I used to feel big and clumsy around him when we were first together. Like I should get small so he would feel bigger. But that went away. We get along okay. I mean most of the time anyway."

"Does he support you, Ellie?"

"Sort of," I said. "I'm living in his house with him and not paying rent or anything. Sometimes I work in the store, like when they expanded into the space next door, or just when it's busy. I take Darby and help out."

"And does he pay you for that help?"

"No," I said. "I'm just helping out. I think it works out. He does a lot of stuff for Darby. And I have income coming in."

She raised her eyebrows in a question.

"From the trust fund Aunt Barbara set up for me. She's a stock broker. She raised me, and she set up a fund a long time ago. So I don't really have to work unless I want to live luxuriously, which I don't usually. Which is why I would like to be able to publish things or sell things or perform."

"And how does Frank feel about your publishing or selling things?"

"I don't know. He doesn't care."

She tilted her head to one side. "He doesn't care."

"He cares about me and Darby. He just doesn't care about what I do." I could hear my voice getting shrill, and I could feel the tears pricking my eyes. She raised her eyebrows at me again. I decided to quit trying to make it better. I wasn't doing a very good job.

"So you are living intimately with this man and working for him, and he's not paying you for your work. Nor does he support your creative life."

"He does," I said, stung back into speech. "He likes my stuff. He just isn't involved in it, it's not his problem."

"Ellie, as women we have been trained to take care of men's business for them without expecting to get paid or having our investment reciprocated. For you to accept that your labor and time aren't worth anything is very erosive of self-esteem, which is at the root of your difficulty. You are going to have to deal with this with Frank. You need to be empowered and this is a first step."

"I can't," I said.

"You can't, or you won't?" she asked.

"What's the difference really?" I was feeling the familiar tears rising up in my chest, sobs wracking my body. "I can't," I said.

"You will," she assured me. "You really will."

"Frank, how come you don't pay me when I work in the store?"

"What?" He looked up from his book, eyes still focused somewhere far away.

"Why don't you pay me wages when I work in the store?"

"How much do you want?"

"I don't know."

"Well, let me know. Also I need your social security number and a W-4 with withholding information."

"It's really important," I said. "It's important to my self-esteem." I was beginning to sound whiny. "It's important to me as a woman."

"Ellie, I didn't know that you felt like that."

"I didn't. Or at least, I didn't know I did."

"Sweetie, just let me know and I'll tell Barney to put you on the books. Okay?"

"Okay," I said. But I never did get around to it.

I had something to tell her, and I hugged it to my chest all the way up the stairs. I knew if I seemed too eager, I wouldn't get to talk about it.

"I had a dream last night that was very disturbing. I dreamed I was in an abandoned city, and there was a woman there who was my guide. She had dark brown hair in braids coiled on her head, very old-fashioned, and she had very pale skin and blue eyes that stuck out. And she seemed very cold and impatient. Very tall."

"That's my mother."

"What?"

"That's my mother."

"No," I said, feeling like someone had smacked me at the base of my skull with an ice bag. "No," I said, "I don't know your mother."

She leaned forward with her elbows on her knees, looking at me intently, and said, "That is a perfect description of my mother."

"No," I said, floundering, "it's not really your mother. I haven't ever met your mother."

She sat back with a bounce and glared at me with defiance, triumph, perhaps even contempt. "That is a perfect physical description of my mother." I goggled at her. "Why do you suppose you are dreaming about my mother? What does that do for you?"

"I don't think I dreamed about your mother." I was watching her face, trying to gauge if this was some kind of therapy trick.

"How are you feeling, Ellie? You seem to be reacting very strongly. Close your eyes, and let's see if you can focus on your feelings."

I couldn't bring myself to close my eyes. My eyes felt round and wary. How did I feel? "I feel scared," I said. "I feel very scared." And saying it out loud, I could feel the wavering overlaid images of my self coalescing. I said it again. "I'm scared." I didn't say, "I have to get out of here."

"Close your eyes," she said. "Tell me about the fear."

I couldn't close my eyes. "I'm blanking out," I said. "I can't feel anything."

She took the three twenty dollar bills I had given her out of the appointment book where she had laid them. She fanned them out like a hand of cards and showed them to me. "What is this?" she said. "Hmmm? This is what you give me every week. What does that mean to you? What are you buying?"

"I don't know," I said. I felt like crying with shame and confusion, but I couldn't. "I don't know. I wanted to be able to do things I can't do."

"You wanted. And what do you want now?"

"I don't know," I said. I wanted to be somewhere

else. I wanted out. When I got home, I threw up.

"Frank, I'm really afraid that my therapist is crazy."

He smiled. Crazy could mean a lot of things, and some of the crazy people we knew were a lot of fun.

"No, I mean really crazy."

"What's up?" he asked.

"She thinks I'm dreaming about her mother."

He stared at me, waiting for the punch line. "Really?"

"Yes."

We sat for a moment. Darby came over and climbed into my lap. I rested my chin on his hard little head with its velvety covering of hair so fine and pale that the individual strands were almost invisible.

"You won't go back then, right? Right, Ellie?"

"I have an appointment."

"You don't have to go back, Ellie. If it's not good for you, if it doesn't help, you don't have to see her."

"What do I tell her? I can't tell her anything."

"You call her answering service and tell them that you are canceling your appointment. You don't have to explain."

"I can't."

We sat for a moment longer.

"Okay, I guess I have to."

* * *

I called the next day. "This is Ellie Pakuchka. I'm going to have to cancel my appointment next week with Patricia. Thursday, four o'clock."

The woman at the other end sniffed. "Do you want to reschedule for the following week?"

"No," I said.

"Are you terminating treatment?" she asked.

"Look," I said, "just cancel my appointment, okay?"

"I'll have Patricia call you back to reschedule."

"No," I said, "don't do that." And I hung up.

Patricia called me the next evening. "My answering service tells me that you are terminating. Don't you think you should discuss that with me?"

I wanted to drop the phone receiver. "I don't know," I said.

"You aren't suicidal" she said, "but I would be very much remiss in my professional responsibility if I failed to warn you that this kind of termination can have very grave repercussions."

I said nothing.

"Ellie, I really urge you to come in and let's talk about this, for your own sake. Let's schedule another session or two to achieve completion of the work you've been doing. It's really important. I don't want to be alarming, and I don't really see you as being at risk. But I strongly urge you to finish what we've been doing."

I was turning to stone, starting at the ear and moving down. Special effects.

"Shall we meet again next week?"

"Okay," I said. "One more session. That's all."

"I'm relieved that you've made that decision. I'll see you then."

"Frank, I'm going back to see Patricia, just for one session to tie up the loose ends."

"I thought you said she was crazy."

"I don't know. It's just one. I couldn't get out of it."

"I can't believe you, Ellie. Don't get hurt. Tell her your boyfriend likes you the way you are. Tell her you've developed an allergy to bullshit. Tell her anything. You don't have to tell the truth, you know. You don't owe her anything. You don't even have to show up."

I went up the stairs as slowly as I could, reminding myself, "This is not a hanging. This is more like a root canal. It won't last forever. I will survive."

"Sorry I'm late." I breezed into the room and sat down, carefully arranging my arms and legs in a casual pose. "I had trouble finding a good parking space. I can't believe what they're doing to the streets."

"So, Ellie, you want to terminate. Tell me about

that."

"I feel that I've learned enough to go on for a while. I'm feeling much stronger and more competent. I have arranged for a few auditions at coffee houses next week, which feels pretty good. I've really improved my relationship with Frank. He's paying me wages like we talked about, and my relationship with Darby is lots better. He's sleeping with a duck now." I had just gone through in thirty seconds all the things I had planned to use to fill the fifty-minute hour. My face was a mask with wary eyes. I was lying through my teeth.

"I'm glad to hear it. I have enjoyed working with you. You have so much potential and creativity. Is there anything you wanted to ask me about the work we've done here?"

Ah, I thought. Keep them talking. I felt like a policeman talking to a suicide, controlling my eyes, trying not to betray the firemen with the net creeping up behind her.

"Yes," I said. "I wondered if you could give me some general feedback. It's so hard for us to see ourselves, and I wondered if you could just tell me how you have seen our work together."

"This is sick," I thought. "I'm going to be sick again."

I could see her talking but I couldn't quite listen to her, and I made my face look placid and interested, hoping my eyes wouldn't give me away. Her heart-shaped face and her pale eyes and hair seemed so familiar and so frightening. "Her nose goes up and down when she talks," I thought. "I wonder why I never noticed that before." I looked around her office surreptitiously, seeing for the first time a green vase with dragons and chrysanthemums painted on it. How can anyone do that by hand? What would an apprentice vase-painter do? Mix paint? Stack vases? All of the dragon but the face? A pair of sunglasses lay next to the vase on the dark wooden table. Is sunlight good for your eyes, or is it harmful? I've read both things. Is it like most things, a matter of degree? Maybe I should buy some sunglasses. The clock is moving very slowly. I felt my gorge rising, and I spoke quickly into a break in the monologue.

"Patricia, I feel kind of sick. I'll be right back." And I sprinted for the floral motif bathroom and lost my lunch into the sparkling clean toilet bowl. I rested my forehead on the edge of the toilet, cold and bracing. It seemed very peaceful and easy to just stay there. After a while, my thighs began to cramp and my knees were hurting from the hard floor. I stood up, washed out my mouth, and went back. It was almost over.

"Okay, I did it."

Frank came around behind me and put his hands

around my waist, pressing his head against my back. "How was it?"

"It was awful. It made me throw up again." I felt tearful and trembly.

He began to nibble the nape of my neck, and his hands went up to cuddle my breasts. "Maybe you're pregnant," he said.

A year later, when my daughter Caitlin began to sleep through the night, I started dreaming that I was locked in a coffin with a white cat that screamed and clawed the wood. I could feel it working its way up the side of the box from my feet toward my head. My arms were confined to my sides. I knew there would be nothing I could do to protect my face and my eyes when it reached that far. I woke up drenched with sweat, and the mood of fear and hopelessness seemed to cling to me during the day. I made an appointment to see someone a friend recommended, a therapist named Marva Downing. As I went up the stairs to her office, I wondered who she would be and if she could help me and if I really needed help.

She was a dark-haired woman, older than me, with shiny brown eyes and glasses.

"What can I do for you, Ellie?" she asked me, her eyebrows up.

"You know," I said, "I feel really scared being here. I feel trapped and scared. I'm afraid I will have to chew my foot off to get out."

She seemed to understand what I was saying. She pointed to the door. "It's not locked, you know. You can leave any time."

"But then I have to come back," I said. "I can't just leave. Because once I leave, that proves I can leave, and then I have to come back."

"You don't have to come back. You can just leave, if that's what you want to do." She smiled at me.

"Okay," I said. And I stood up and walked to the door, pulled it open and stepped out. I felt as though sirens might go off up and down the hall, but it was quiet out there. I turned and looked back in through the doorway at the stranger in the office. She looked quite calm and perhaps a little amused.

"Thanks!" I said and went down the stairs, through the outer door and into the sunshine, a free woman.

And since then I've been fine, except for this dream I've been having. I keep finding pairs of kittens, striped, crayon-colored, rectangular kittens in my sock drawer, behind the couch, all over my house. It doesn't bother me, really, but I'd like to know what it means.

Seraphim, Cherubim, and Sally

"I don't know," Sally said. "I'm not very good at parties." She was already dressed, but having second thoughts. "Maybe you should just go on without me. You'll have a better time that way. It's all your recovery friends."

"Oh, come on," Damien said. "It's a long drive down there, and people will think it's strange if I show up alone. I mean, we're supposed to be a couple again. People know you're back. And you say you want to be supportive."

"I do. Of course I do. Just don't abandon me when we get there, okay? Like, hang around a little?"

"Abandon," he mocked her. "Abandon. I'm asking you to go to a party with me and my friends, and you start accusing me before we get out the door."

"I won't know anybody there," Sally said. "They're all new." Sally caught herself starting to chew on her new scarlet manicure and jammed her hands in her pockets.

"Sam and Judith will be there. You said you liked Judith." The patience in Damien's voiced sounded forced, as though he were about to snap in the new way he had.

" I like her okay. I don't really know her."

"Is that what you're going to wear?" She should have known he would object. Everything had to be so straight now that he was in recovery. He used to be up for anything. He used to think she was gorgeous when he was plastered, showing her off to his friends.

"This here is the most beautiful woman in the universe," he used to say to everyone, weaving a little as she coaxed him out the door. "And she's going home with me."

"I can change," she said. "I haven't unpacked all the way yet." She seemed to be doing everything wrong.

"What happened to your eyes?"

He had nudged her from in front of the mirror in their tiny bathroom while she had been applying her makeup, so she knew his question was rhetorical. She knew she shouldn't be so thin-skinned. He was trying.

"You're stalling," Damien said. "Let's go," and he jangled the keys as though that would make her move faster, like getting a golden retriever excited about a ride in the car.

From the parking lot they could hear the music,

and Sally's spirits rose a little. Maybe there would be dancing. Maybe Damien would dance her around the room like he used to, but it seemed unlikely. Maybe there would be the free-for-all kind of dancing where everybody dances at once, men and women and little children, and people smile at each other. She followed her husband across the parking lot and up the stairs. The dark interior was filled with people and conversation. She followed him to an empty place on a low couch and sank into it till her knees were at the level of her eyes, forming a sort of natural barrier between her and the festivities. Next to her sat Joey and Annie, who smiled and said hi. Sally couldn't think of anything to say, but she smiled nicely and made eye contact.

"Do you want a drink?"

"Sure," she said. "Maybe a coke or something."

Damien pushed off from the swampy couch and moved across the room to the open kitchen space, where he was immediately engaged in conversation by Sam, his new best buddy and sponsor, who pressed a can into his hand. Sally didn't see anyone she knew, so she turned back to Joey and Annie to ask after their kids. Annie answered briefly, in her sweet, empty little voice. Sally knew that they had been married for at least ten years, had five kids, and yet Annie hardly looked eighteen. She reminded Sally of the Madame Alexander dolls of her childhood, black hair, bright

179

blue eyes, and white skin with pale pink cheeks that looked hand-painted. Joey was sitting sideways, gazing at her with the gooney expression of a sixteen-year-old lover. His hand was clasped possessively on the nape of her delicate neck. He murmured to her softly and she sat and smiled.

Sally peered past the standing bodies in the dark room towards the kitchen just in time to see her husband and Sam slip down the hall together. She wanted to follow them.

"Hey, pretty lady."

Sally looked up from the depths of the couch and was glad to see Jonesy with his girlfriend, Renee. She hoped she might be able to get some conversation going after all, though she was pretty sure the reason he called her "pretty lady" was not because of her looks, but because he couldn't remember her name.

"Hi, Jonesy. Hi, Renee."

Jonesy was immediately swept up into the middle of the room and Sally was left with Renee looking down at her with large, golden eyes. If it was possible for a toad to be beautiful, it would look like Renee.

"Having a hard time?" she asked.

"Well," Sally said, "I don't really know many people."

"I used to feel like that," Renee drawled, "before I worked on my self-esteem issues. It's really just a question of…"

Jonesy was motioning to Renee wildly from the other side of the room, and when she saw him, she wheeled around and her face transformed from a contemptuous mask into a beaming smile. She worked her way towards him and the tall, leggy woman he was talking to.

Sally looked around. The room was really packed now. Joey was still gazing at his cute little wife, and his hand was moving about on her neck, touching her finely modeled ears and fingering the curling tendrils that escaped from her ponytail.

"So," said a voice from the floor on the other side of her, "What do you do?"

"I don't know," Sally said stupidly. "Oh, I guess you mean for a living." She laughed. All she could see of the speaker was the light from the kitchen reflected on his big glasses. "I'm an auditor."

He shrank back as though she had said "undertaker" or "executioner."

"It's okay," Sally said. "I don't work for the IRS or anything. I'm not that kind of auditor."

His smile seemed to blink and go out. Perhaps she should have claimed to be a free-lance leper.

"So," Sally said, "what about you? What do you do?"

He didn't seem to hear her. Apparently she had become inaudible. He had turned to the person on the other side of him. Sally checked herself to be sure she was still there.

"I guess I'll go empty my bladder," she said to the party in general, just to see if any of the throng of people around her was actually within earshot. She felt a desire to do something outrageously difficult to ignore, but squelched the impulse. She didn't want to embarrass him in front of his friends. Things were bad enough.

Sally's biggest problem was getting out of the couch. There was a pair of legs jammed up against her knees, and she wasn't going to be able to stand up without clinging to the owner of those legs. She had a flash memory of clinging to her mother's legs in a cold building, crying. But Sally's a big girl now, she reminded herself.

She found a way up by gently pressing her knees against one side of the legs until they moved slightly and she was able, by moving her bottom sideways up the slope of the seat, to scale the couch by degrees and rise to her feet. When she straightened her knees, she was startlingly close to two strangers who were shouting at each other about Acapulco.

Sally worked her way down the hall and waited for her turn, leaning against the wall and hoping she looked casual and poised. Finally the bathroom door opened and a red-faced man emerged, holding a woman by the hand. They both looked angry. There must be a story there.

It was cool in the bathroom, and it was a relief to be alone. It was a relief to pee. She wanted to stay there, maybe have a nice, long shower, but she knew it wouldn't be manners. Her face in the mirror was strained and unfamiliar. Nothing of interest in the medicine cabinet. Stands to reason—clean and sober.

Emerging from the bathroom, Sally noticed Sam and Jonesy in a small bedroom at the end of the dark hall, laughing and listening to her husband, who was sitting in a high-backed satin chair in a circle of light. She could only see the top of his head and his big, padded hands moving in time with his story. She felt like a little match girl, looking in from the cold and dark, or like the family dog, shut out of the living room because the Christmas tree is set up. She wanted to drop to all fours and crawl in unobtrusively, crouching next to his chair, hoping that one of those familiar hands would drop down onto her head and absent-mindedly begin to pet her. In the old days, she used to complain that he manhandled her, couldn't get enough hugs and kisses. Now he seemed to keep a precise distance, like he had a bad sunburn or like she had an invisible contagious plague.

Sally wandered sadly back to the living room, moving toward her still empty place on the couch. She saw that Annie now had her tiny bare feet planted in her husband's lap. He lifted one and placed a kiss on the soft flesh of her instep. Sally changed course and went out the door into the sweet night air, down the stairs and she didn't start crying till she was in the car.

She had been such a fool. When her friends had taken her to Donovan's to celebrate her twenty-first birthday and her newly acquired ability to drink legally using her own ID, Damien had been there, easily, to her eye, the best-looking man in the room, the most fun, the best dancer, the shiniest eyes, the strongest arms. When they danced, she let herself be swept into his solid embrace and nestled there. He made her laugh—he made everyone laugh, his face bright with mischief and whiskey. Coming as she did from a straight-laced Methodist family, this careless hilarity seemed like a glimpse of the promised land, one to which she was drawn and to which she gave her heart completely. She was thrilled when he asked her instead any of the other girls he had charmed to drive him home. There he kissed her and passed out on the couch, but she was still there in the morning, waiting to be loved, and he loved her. She felt like the luckiest girl in the world. Six months later, after she graduated and found a job, they married amid a shower of champagne and good wishes.

Damien drank.

So?

Lots of people drink.

"You're my rock," he would say to her every time she called in sick for him, met him at the emergency room in the early hours, him still reeling, met him at the city lock-up and paid his bail, took him home, arranged for new insurance, got the car towed away, bought a new one, drove him to work, then to occasional job interviews after he was finally fired.

"You're my girl," he said when she took on a second job to pay the household bills, when she made refreshments for poker nights and the Super Sunday bash each year, when she included cases of beer and fifths of whiskey on her grocery list, when she brought him his nightcap.

"My little love," he said, as she maneuvered his heavy, unbalanced body once again through another barroom door, with the blurry voices of his drinking buddies raised in farewell, steered him down the street and into their most recent and cheapest car yet.

And because she loved him, because she was a rock, because he was still handsome, still loved her and made her laugh, she was strong and kept their life going.

But given time, in this case eight years, and enough friction, even charisma rubs thin and affection erodes. Sally began to dread the future stretched out ahead of her with this monkey on her back, this dancing bear at the end of her chain, and she began to suggest, then ask, then beg him to stop, just for this once. Just stay home. Just have a coke. Just have two or three beers. And he would say he would, but he wouldn't. The days of joyful inebriation and rosy infatuation were over.

She left him and went back to her hometown, ostensibly to help her mother move to senior housing, but she knew the marriage was over. She mailed him a note saying that she couldn't live with him as long as he was drinking. Damien called every night for a week, crying and drunk, and she hung up on him.

But when he called four months later, it was different. He had sixty days sobriety, he said. He wanted to make amends to her. He wanted her to come home.

"I'm different," he said. "I've changed. Come home and let's try again." She missed him. She said okay, quit the job she had just started, and went back to him.

He greeted her first with open arms and then, it seemed to her, with suspicion, then a barrage of criticism. She was back in a life she couldn't manage, but this time with no jokes, and she had gone from being his rock to being a pebble in his shoe, an irritant, always wrong, and he was the hero of the story, making his journey to recovery. No wonder she failed the party test, and sat with her face in her hands in the front seat of this brand-new car, bought because he deserved it for working so hard, and cried her heart out.

Sally was a very good crier, having had a lot of practice. But crying doesn't last forever, even when it seems like it will. She finally stopped, lowering her window and letting the soft, cool air in. She blew her nose on a paper towel from the glove compartment and sat back, wondering, "What the hell am I doing? What am I doing with my life? Why can't I make this work? What am I doing here alone in this damn parking lot?"

"Taking some time out?" a mild voice asked. Sally turned and saw Judith, Sam's wife, standing there, her frilly white blouse gleaming in the low light, two-year-old son Christopher balanced on one hip. Her round, freckled face was friendly and curious.

"Yeah," Sally said, sniffing surreptitiously. "Just taking some time out."

"I just dropped by to say hi to folks," Judith said. "I don't really like parties that much, not my thing, so Sam and I came in different cars."

Christopher waved one stubby arm around toward the other side of the parking lot. "Sa da-ee cah!" he proclaimed, and fixed Sally with a blue stare.

"You saw your daddy's car?" she asked.

He nodded solemnly. His body trembled like a little motor starting up. He leaned toward her. "Da-ee cah weh!" He sat back against his mother and waited expectantly for Sally's response.

"Daddy's car is red," she said. "You saw your daddy's red car." Christopher continued to attach her with his eyes.

"What color is your momma's car?" Sally asked.

His eyes focused inwardly and after a moment, he smiled with triumph and pronounced, "Boo!"

"Momma has a blue car."

"This is great," said Judith, and her warm hand rested for a moment on Sally's night-cooled arm, then went back to steady the baby. "At the party, people kept asking Christopher questions, and then when he answered, they'd look at me and say 'What is he saying?' This is really great."

Christopher leaned so far towards Sally that his mother had to move forward to keep him balanced. He seemed to want to put his forehead against Sally's, to join at the brain. He struggled with another statement, his breath making a hiccing sound as he inhaled twice between words. His face was blazing with the intense effort of using words. "Ma," he said, "ma boo too buff."

It was an exciting game, and Sally's concentration was fierce now. "You have a blue toothbrush," she half-guessed, but the moment she said it she knew she was right.

He opened his rosy mouth, tilting his head back to show her his teeth in confirmation. In the half-light of the parking lot, Sally couldn't see them, but she knew they were there. Then he lost interest, and his round head dropped heavily against Judith's shoulder.

"I'd better get this kid home to bed," Judith said. She touched Sally's arm again briefly, and the streetlights shone behind her aureole of curls and her fluttering, white blouse as she moved away. Her soft "good-night" floated behind her.

Sally breathed in peacefully. The air carried a soft flowery scent into the car, and she could hear the beginning sputter of automatic sprinklers turning themselves on, followed by the smell of wet grass. She leaned her back against the car-door, resting her feet in the driver's seat. She was cool and tired, her mind a field of emptiness, and eventually she dozed off and dreamed of butterflies.

When the door on the driver's side opened with a jerk, Sally instinctively pulled back her feet.

"Get your feet off of the seat. Jesus Christ, where have you been? What's wrong with you?" Damien glared at her, but what she saw on his face looked like fear, as though he had half expected to find the car empty and her gone.

"Nothing," she said, gently scratching her itchy shoulder blades against the rough upholstery. "Nothing is wrong with me."

He closed the car door and fastened his seatbelt, a newly acquired habit.

"I looked all over for you, and you just disappeared. What do you think you're doing out here? You just embarrassed the hell out of me, you know that?"

Sally felt like she could see through his words to a vision of all the times he had shouted and danced and thrown up and fallen down and destroyed furniture and wrecked cars and started fistfights with other drunks, the shame he had not felt at the time coming back now in full force when he had no way to protect himself from it. She had felt her own embarrassments then and there and had nothing left over to suffer.

"I took some time out," Sally said. "I don't much like parties, so I'm taking a break."

He snorted and started the car, jamming it into reverse. She reached over and turned the car off.

"Here's the deal," she said. "If we don't like each other, we can't stay married. Not that we have to agree all the time. But if you want me to stay with you, you have be nice. To me."

"What is that supposed to mean? That I'm not nice? What about you?"

She just repeated, "If we're going to stay married, we have to like each other. And you have to be nice to me or I can't stay."

"I don't think you know," he said, "how hard I'm working to recover. Some really bad feelings come up. I don't think you understand."

"I read your Big Book, you know, like you asked me to, at least most of it. And I didn't see anywhere that you can't be nice to your wife."

"I'm scared," he said. "I don't know who I am anymore. I feel like my skin is gone."

"Okay," Sally said. "Tell me that, tell me whatever you need to. You don't have to tell me anything you don't want to, or what you just tell your sponsor or your meetings. If you need time alone, say so. If you need my company, ask for it. Do whatever it takes to get better. But when you do talk to me, be nice."

"What makes you so special and perfect? What makes you God's gift to mankind?" he asked, and would have said more, but her stillness made it clear she was not going to fight. He saw that she was smiling at him. "You can't understand what I'm going through." His voice trailed off.

"Probably not, but I have other places I can be. I left a job to come back to be with you, to try again. It has to work for me, too."

"You have to work on your character defects too, then. It's not just about me. Recovery means the whole family. Read the section on 'To the Wives.'"

"My character defects are not your problem, not even your business, Damien. I don't want your criticisms. If you don't like me, I have others places I can be. Be nice—that's all."

"So now you're holding yourself hostage, exploiting my abandonment issues?"

"Bottom line, Damien," she said, counting out the three sentences on her fingers. "I have other places to be. We have to like each other. Be nice to me."

"And don't drink," he added.

Sally held up a fourth finger. "Don't drink," she agreed.

They fell silent, and Sally didn't know what would happen next. She felt light-hearted for the first time in years, relaxed in a new way that made her smile and enjoy the cool air on her face. They drove home in silence, and she felt that Damien was driving calmly, almost gently, as he eased them into the stream of cars. Yes and no swirled in the air between them like a pair of butterflies, and she saw in the headlights of oncoming traffic that his eyes were bright with tears, though she didn't know what he wept for. Pain, acceptance, confusion, hope, letting go of hope, grief, love, all seemed to be made of the same fabric, and she didn't have to know. Tonight she was content. She had been visited by angels. She had spoken in their tongue. More would be revealed.

Donna's Story

Of course, there's a first time for everything, like you say, and this was mine. I was a sophomore in high school, and I went to the Spring Fling with my best friend Sandy Hanson. Usually if you went to a dance with just other girls, you didn't dress up that much, but for some reason we did that time. I had a frilly pink dress my sister had handed down and some white shoes with pink flowers on them that didn't go with anything else I owned. And usually you just watched and saw who was dancing with who and talked. But this time was different because there were three or four guys who kept asking us to dance and shoving each other around, and we felt kind of popular, which wasn't how it usually went, at least with me.

So one of these guys had black hair and lots of hair on his chest, and he was quite a good-looking kind of guy, in a way. I really wanted him to like me, so when we danced a slow dance, which in those days was just smack up cheek-to-cheek, belly-to-belly dancing, I let him hold me real close. He smelled kind of good and kind of too strong. Nowadays, I put a lot of stock in how a man smells, but I couldn't begin to explain it. Just some men smell good and others don't. If you want a good man, you find one that smells good to you. I don't mean shaving lotion and stuff like that. I mean the man himself.

So anyhow, we danced and he called me "Baby" which made me feel stirred up inside. Nobody had ever called me that before, just songs on the radio. Oh, Baby mine. I don't think I'd ever danced with a boy with hair on his chest before. My hands were so sweaty, I wondered if I was leaving wet handprints on his back for all the world to see. I looked over, and I saw Sandy's face over the shoulder of the guy she was dancing with. Her eyes were closed and she looked very romantic.

After the dance, Sandy and her guy Brett came over, and Sandy and I went to the bathroom to talk. I was almost afraid to leave, because it seemed like the guy might forget about me and go outside with a group of guys or something, or dance with someone else and call them baby. But I went, and we peed and then started fixing our hair. That was a job. Sandy helped me rat my hair. That's where you take a hank of it in your hand and run backwards down it with a comb, and it makes a snarl, and you comb the top layer over the ratted part, and it makes it poofy. That's how we did it. Then I washed my hands with cold water, hoping that the cold would stay in them, and I wouldn't embarrass myself if I got a chance to hold hands or something.

Sandy was laughing about something. One of the guys who wasn't dancing had a car, but the windows had gotten broken, and somehow this guy, Brett, had made that seem real funny to Sandy. I didn't get it, but I guess you had to be there. Sandy wanted me and the guy I was dancing with to go with her and Bret in the car, just out to the mesa outside town. I was shocked. "You mean to PARK?" She was trying to sound casual, like this was something she did all the time. "Just to hang out. Y'know, to talk and stuff."

I was supposed to be home by 11:30. My parents always set curfews like that for me, even though I usually got home early. My sister used to go out a lot in high school, and they hadn't noticed yet that I was always home. I'd be going out the door to get something I was borrowing from Sandy which was two doors down from us, and they'd yell "Now you be home by" whatever it was. I would have thought it was funny, but I tended to take things like that personal, and I wished they would have noticed that it was me, and that I going to be home in minutes and that I never went anywhere worth staying up late for.

I did have this curfew, but somehow I didn't feel like it applied to me, and it was only 10:00 or so. So I thought, well, why not? I would like to be in the dark under the stars with a guy some day, and it seemed like as good a chance as I was likely to get. Being called baby had made me feel like I was something special, and that made me reckless. So Sandy and I talked it out, and I decided that I owed it to myself to go, and anyway, if I didn't go, Sandy couldn't. At least that's what she said. So I said I would.

We went back out to the dance, and Brett and the other guy were waiting for us. So we got our jackets and stuff and went out the door. I hoped that a lot of people were watching and wondering just what we were up to. I was hoping that this was when I would start to get noticed and popular.

So we got into the car, Sandy and Brett in the front, and me and the other boy in the back seat. I said, "I don't believe I even know your name." And he said, "Chuck." That seemed like a shame. I don't remember what I thought was a really great name for a guy, but that wasn't it. He sat real close by me, pushing me into the door handle a little bit, and he held my hand. He was humming something very quietly. It seemed like a movie to me. And for once, I was the one who was at the center of things.

We headed somewhere out on the mesa. Sandy and Bret were talking about Mr. Spitzer, which was easy to do, because he was almost the weirdest teacher at our school. They were laughing, and she was sitting just even with the rear view mirror, not all scrunched together like I was. It sounded like they were having a lot more fun than us. But then Chuck put his right arm all the way around my shoulders and gave me a little squeeze. And his left hand put my left hand on his right leg, and he started to put his left hand on my breast. Well, he hadn't even kissed me, and I was pretty sure that I was supposed to do something. So I leaned forward real quick and yelled out "Boy, did you see Mr. Spitzer when Terry Whitlow got the chalk hand-prints all over his rear end?" They laughed at that, but when I went to scoot back in the seat, Chuck had made it so that I was practically sitting on his lap. I was beginning to feel kind of cornered, and I felt like if he was going to be interested in me, he had better kiss me. That was what I expected. I thought that was what boys wanted.

After a while we got to wherever it was we were going, and after the car engine stopped ringing in our ears, we listened to the silence, which got pretty intense after a while. Chuck put his face down into my neck, which made the hair on my arms stand up, and said "Let's go for a walk, Baby," and I said "Oh, no, let's just stay here for a while." Then I realized that Sandy and Brett were getting out of the car, and I was going to be left alone with Chuck, which was what I was trying to avoid, but I didn't see how I could change my mind. So

Sandy and Brett stumbled off into the dark, and then Chuck really started in on me.

He had his hands all over my dress, and then inside my dress, and it didn't take me too long to realize that he was trying to get my dress all the way off. I didn't know how long Sandy and Bret were going to be gone, but I certainly hadn't intended to undress in front of anyone. I tried to push him away, and I asked him to stop, which I remember was what they said to do at Christian Youth Group when things were going too far. He said "Baby, you got me going, and I can't stop now." He was so hot it was uncomfortable to touch him and sweaty and everywhere at once, it seemed like. I really didn't want to, but I had never expected to be in a situation like that, and I didn't want to be rude. He had my dress off by then, and hooked his thumb in my underwear and pulled that off like he was an expert or something, and it was almost like I was two people by then, one of them looking on, kind of interested and calm, and one real scared and excited.

Well, it hurt. In fact, it hurt a lot because it was the very first time, and he just pushed into me until he was all the way in. I don't know if it hurts that way for everyone. Anyway, the calm, looking-on person heard the scared and excited one actually scream. It was entirely unexpected.

I really didn't know what to expect. I had been

told in first grade that the guy puts his thing in the girl's thing. Well, it sounds silly now, but that's what they said. I don't think I really believed it till a lot later. I had assumed that there was a lot of other stuff, but I wasn't sure what it was. Like in the movies, when the picture gets foggy, and that's the love scene. Or in books I'd read, where all of a sudden after they kissed and felt passionate it was the next morning. I'd had a few foggy dreams of my own. But I didn't know what to expect. So there I was with Chuck in somebody's car, and my privates hurt, and he was grunting and sweating and calling me baby, but I wasn't liking it anymore. Still I felt tender towards him in a funny way, he was so close. But I was hoping that he would stop pretty soon, and I could get my clothes on before Sandy and Bret got back.

After a while, he did stop, and then he just held me and kissed my eyelids and my neck and ran his fingers down my face, and smoothed my hair off my forehead, and he just looked at me for the longest time, studying my face like a picture. We stayed like that a long time, and I felt like time had stopped and that everything would be different from now on. I finally got my clothes back on, and then Sandy and Bret came staggering back to the car, giggling and holding hands. I felt like I lived in a different world and I didn't know what it was.

When we got to my house, it was 1:30. Chuck walked me up the sidewalk and kissed me goodnight. I was hoping that he would say something, but he didn't. I didn't know what was going to happen with my folks, but the porch light was on and the door was unlocked like we did then and they were asleep, so it was okay. I felt like I might have enjoyed blowing off some steam with one of those scenes like my sister used to have when she got home late, but it was very quiet.

My parents never seemed to know how late I had been out. I never saw Chuck again. When I went over to talk to Sandy the next day, and I really needed a friend, she was all giggly and sly, talking about Brett, what he said and did, how cute he was, so I lied and said we just made out. She acted like she was in on some kind of delicious secret, like she had robbed the cookie jar, but I just couldn't see it that way. What I saw was how much who I was didn't matter in the world, and it took a long time after that night for me to learn what mattered to me, what I wanted out of the deal. They call it the loss of innocence. Is that what it sounds like to you? I guess if innocence means believing lies.

The funny thing about that night is, when I was stumbling through the dark living room, trying not to bump into the furniture, I heard Cap, my dad's German Shepherd, moving around in the garage. I went and opened the door for him to come in. He just stood there in the cold, car-smelling dankness, even when I called him in a whisper. He wasn't allowed in the house much, and didn't seem to want to break the rules like I did, like I just had done. I doubled back to the kitchen and got a box of vanilla wafers to use. He ate the first one, and then followed me through the dark house, just stopping a little at the turn in the hallway. He had never been past that point, but it only took two more vanilla wafers to get him the rest of the way.

Inside my room, I closed the door and tried to get Cap to jump up on the bed. In the end, I had to hoist his hind end up and give him several cookies in a row to stop him from jumping back down. I petted him and it was funny how uncomfortable he was. I would have thought he wanted in where it was warm with the soft bed under him instead of the cold cement floor that made calluses on his elbows. He liked the petting, and the cookies even more, and it was like some kind of game to see if I could get him to relax and go to sleep. I ate a few vanilla wafers myself and then I lay on the bed with my arm over his warm shoulders, my hand holding his rough front paw, and fell asleep. I felt him leave me some time later and heard him sigh as he found a spot mashed up against the closed door to finish out the night.

A Perfectly
Good Marriage

I can picture Cindy now, some years later, her red hair in a crazy ponytail, talking to some guy who's not me in a bar, some guy maybe better looking than me, though that wouldn't be anything remarkable. She would be smoking a menthol cigarette, but maybe she's quit like she was always trying to do. Either way, I suppose her and this guy are sniffing around each other, him hoping to get lucky and get laid and her hoping to get incredibly lucky and have him fall in love with her and be the one who makes her dreams come true. I'm not saying that couldn't happen. She's a good-looking girl, woman now I guess, and when she smiles her eyes shine in a way that makes you forget what you were thinking about, just for a minute or two. And her laugh has a deep, bouncy sound to it that makes you remember where your belly is and makes you start thinking about what other kinds of noises she might make under different circumstances.

I met Cindy when I was twenty and she was nineteen. We hooked up when she got dumped by my best friend Manny, who took off for Alaska with some woman he just met. So I gave her a shoulder to cry on, I told her what a great girl she was, and she really was, and that Manny was a horse's ass for treating her like that. I should have heard a prophetic voice echoing in my head when I said those words, horse's ass.

Stubborn runs in my family, I now realize, though when I was twenty, I thought it was just my dad. I thought of stubborn as some fool notion my dad would get and my mom and us kids would shake our heads over. Now I am told I'm just as pigheaded. According to a number of ladies and employers I have known, self-knowledge has not cured me of this failing. "It's like you think you're nailed to the ground," Cindy once told me, "and everyone else has to work around you."

So this guy I'm imagining, this lucky guy, sitting on a barstool, turned to watch my ex-wife's pretty face, to run his presuming eyes all over her, he'd be making the kind of small talk that is trying to end up in bed. He'd buy her a drink or two, as many as she'd have. He'd ask her, at some point, and this is the point I'm dreading, if she had ever been married. She wouldn't be in a hurry to answer. She'd put something in her mouth, maybe a cherry or a slice of lime, and he wouldn't care if she ever answered, just for watching her suck on it.

Of course for all I know, she's been married two or three times by now, gained a hundred pounds, has five kids, is the first female deacon of the Methodist church, not hanging out in bars talking to good-time joes. But that's where I picture her, there at the bar, turning her face to him, giving him the full benefit of her bright blue eyes, and telling him why she divorced her husband and what a good idea that had turned out to be. She would just say it straight out, tell him that she divorced her husband over a bag of potato chips.

And it would be true, or true enough. They would have to take their drinks over to a table together then, so she could explain it better, and if he had any sense, he'd ask if she wanted a bar snack. I imagine her waving away the offer. "Thanks," she would say, "I'm not hungry right now." He would prod her to tell the story, and two states away, my big ears would start to burn and I'd feel a shiver like a whole gaggle of geese were congregating on my grave, full of evil intent like they are.

It's not a complicated story. We were in my old red truck driving back from Flagstaff, where I had gone to meet up with a friend of mine named Dave who was in the contracting business there, hoping to get either some work from him, though I'd have to crash somewhere local if I did, or some grass, if he was still in that line of business. It was pretty much nothing doing in both departments. Double nothing. The years had not improved either his personality or his character, though his luck appeared to have taken an upturn. All he could talk about was his rich fiancée who had some Spanish princess name like Carmen or Maria or something. We had lunch with him at Denny's, and he didn't even pick up the tab, even with all the good fortune he was so sure he deserved.

Cindy and I had been married for a few years at that point, just a quick trip to the JP so I could get coverage on her medical that she got at work. We had both been a little hung-over, so it wasn't exactly the wedding day a girl dreams about. The way Dave was talking about his upcoming wedding made me feel pretty small and plain, and I could see that Cindy was bored. She had that flat look she gets when I would try to talk to her about drywall or asphalt or even power tools. If she could fly, she would have been long gone, but there she was between us in the booth, so she couldn't just slip out to look at postcards or the jukebox selections. She was not in the sweetest mood, but then I wasn't having much fun either. She just poked at her salad like she was looking for a wing nut she had dropped and not finding it.

We finally found a space between the honeymoon in the Bahamas and the new job with his rich father-in-law in which we could just interject our congratulations on his impressive life and get away. It's a long drive back to Phoenix, a mostly long dry road we had already driven that morning when we had enjoyed the scenery for what it was worth, but it was less entertaining and less scenic after a long pointless bout of listening to Dave admire himself. I just wanted to get home and smoke a joint or two to mellow out. Cindy sat over by the window on the passenger side, smoking and staring out at the nothing on the roadside, mile after mile.

"You know," she said, "I'm really hungry. How about you pull over at the next little place we see and I'll get some potato chips or something. I think there's a gas station in a mile or two."

"We're not stopping," I said. "It's only a little over an hour and we'll be home. We've got groceries in the house." I punched some buttons on the stereo panel, looking for something besides preachers to listen to. "We just had lunch."

"Hey," she said. "I'm really really hungry. I need food. I need you to stop so I can get something to eat."

"We're not stopping," I said.

We both saw the little gas station at about the same time, on the right just a little further on at the next exit, and I set my jaw and kept my foot steady on the accelerator. Cindy turned so that her back was to the door and stared at me, as though eye-power was going to turn the steering wheel and take us to the parking lot of the run-down joint where her magic potato chips were waiting for her. Sixty miles-per-hour straight ahead, not even a swerve in that direction.

"You son of a bitch," she said. "Why didn't you stop? It would only take a minute or two."

"We'll be home in an hour, maybe less," I said, sounding pretty reasonable I thought.

"Stop at the bar then," she said, "the one on the other side of the overpass, with the Paul Bunyan statue in front. Stop there."

"Don't hold your breath," I said. "It's not going to kill you to wait till we get home, less than an hour. You're not starving to death."

"If you don't stop at that bar so I can get some potato chips," she said, "I'm going to divorce you."

That just about floored me—divorce over a little thing like that? A seventy-nine-cent bag of potato chips?

"Is that all our marriage means to you?" I asked. "A piddly little bag of potato chips?"

"Is that all it means to you?" she shot back. "Can't stop for five minutes? Can't suit anyone but yourself?"

"It's the principle of the thing," I said. "I'm not going to be blackmailed into doing whatever fancy comes into your head. We've got stuff at home to eat.

We'll be there in less than an hour."

"If you were hungry," she said, "we'd stop for sure. If you wanted to stop, we'd stop."

"I'm driving," I said, "and there's no point stopping so close to home."

"You're always driving."

"That's right," I said. "It's my truck. And the reason I wouldn't want to stop is because I ate my lunch instead of playing with it."

"I'm hungry," she said. "I want you to stop at that bar. If you won't do that for me, I'm going to divorce you. That's all."

We whizzed past The Lumberjack at closer to seventy miles per hour, not even in the right-hand lane, I was that put out with her unreasonable attitude.

"That's just the stupidest thing I ever heard," I said. "Breaking up a perfectly good marriage over something so petty. That's the word for it. Petty."

"Nevertheless," she said. And that was all she said, not even commenting when we passed a number of other stores and fast food places on the outskirts of town. That was the last word she said to me. Nevertheless. I have a hard time now wrapping my head around what that means.

As soon as we got home and pulled into the driveway, she slid out of the truck and left the door hanging open. When I got inside, she was already scrambling some eggs in a skillet with her right hand and munching on a chunk of cheese in her left.

"You go easy on those eggs," I said. "Too much eggs can cause cholesterol." I was just looking out for her, but she gave me that flat stare. I drank a few beers and smoked the first half of the last joint in my possession, watching a rerun of The Price is Right on television and ignoring the way she was ignoring me. I can have a pretty good time with just those simple things, something to get a buzz on and something to space out with. I could hear her rummaging around in the bedroom, but I was trying to rise above it all, figuring she'd get off her high horse soon enough.

It must have been while I was in the john that she dragged her suitcase through the living room and loaded it into the truck. And then she drove off, leaving me high and dry, with no wheels except her dinky little Tercel and no wife at all. I called the highway patrol, figuring it would put a scare into her to get pulled over, but the lady on the phone said it's a community property state, and a person can't steal what already belongs to them.

"It's my truck," I said. "You can't take a man's truck."

"You're married?" she asked.

"We may be married," I said, "but she can't just take her husband's work truck like that."

"She can in Arizona," the lady said, and she didn't

sound very sorry about it either.

Cindy didn't ever come back. I thought the guys down at the Pioneer Lounge would shake their heads over how unreasonable she was, how unreasonable they all are, make some jokes about PMS, buy me a drink or two. I thought they would, but they just laughed.

Skinny, the bartender, laughed so hard he almost cracked his head on the bar.

"Why didn't you just buy her the damn potato chips?" he asked. "Why not?"

I started to repeat that we were less than an hour from home and all the other reasons that had made so much sense to me at the time. But I could see that the sooner I quit talking about it, the better. Evidently I didn't drop it soon enough, since it got to be the big joke whenever I was there. I came real close to getting thrown out one night when Bobby Lee started calling me Chip instead of my name. I took a swing at him and broke his nose, which put an end to that particular line of comedy. Still, the sale of potato chips must have tripled after that, guys innocently asking for Ranch or BBQ, making sure I could hear them, snickering at all the clever things they could think up to say about potato chips.

I quit going there for a while, to let it die down and something else come up to be the big joke at the Pioneer. I didn't even tell them when I got the divorce

211

papers from California, to be returned to a post office box, although that was about the darkest day of my life. I was too low to even get drunk. I just signed it and spent the rest of the day in bed, doubled up like I had appendicitis again.

But there it is, that's the story she'll tell him, that I wouldn't stop for potato chips, and I imagine him making a decision in the back of his head to get what he could for tonight and then cut loose from the crazy woman, one who would take something like a bag of potato chips so personal. I imagine him seeing the reason on my side of the argument and thinking he would have done the same thing.

But then maybe what I imagine isn't what happens. Maybe what happens is the kind of thing she would imagine, that this would be a man who would fall in love with her and do all the things guys do in the movies to prove it. He would hold her sweet face between gentle hands and kiss her gently and promise to do things that would make her happy whether they made any sense or not, because her being happy was his aim in life. I can imagine the glow of her skin with that kind of man.

She's long gone, and no amount of thinking is going to bring her back. But I think if she came back to me, I would give her as many potato chips as she wanted, whenever she wanted them. I would stop the truck every two miles all the way home from anywhere. I'd work night and day to pay for anything she wanted. If that was potato chips, so be it. I'd fill up the bathtub with potato chips, and she could lay in them naked and look at me with that pleased, sly look of a willing woman trading looks with a man she intends to have. I can almost taste it.

Wayne's Left Hand

The Parkinson's disease seminar filled the main auditorium of the Masonic temple. Long tables were set off-kilter, like the stripes in a chevron, so that attention was directed to the stage in the center front. Large screens on each side of the podium threatened PowerPoint. Each weak or rigid or shuffling or trembling or limping or gesticulating participant seemed to be accompanied by a tired, hopelessly cheerful caregiver. Eyes darted about to assess the deterioration, the mental state, the predictive lifespan of each symptom-bearing casualty.

The doctor's voice boomed into the hall, making Cheryl's ears crackle. Surely he would step back, or someone would move the microphone away from his healthy, aggressive voice box or turn the volume down. On her right, Wayne pulled his tiny tin box from his pocket, withdrew two earplugs, and pushed them into his ears—dexterously on the right side, less so on the left. Wayne was prepared. His voice, when they had been deciding whether or not to attend this event, had been just a little thready, with starts and stops, like water arising reluctantly from a rusty pump.

"It's a way to get the big picture," he had argued.

Cheryl was not sure she could bear the big picture, but he was usually right, had usually been right.

She had not known what to expect at the seminar, but the distance between the care professionals and the suffering seemed greater than she had thought it would be. She realized that she had expected sympathy. She was looking, not for information, but for an escape route. The doctor's voice still gushed out into the room, and Cheryl held her ears shut with both hands and tried to listen.

As she strained to keep her mind focused on the names of drugs—Mirapex, Sinemet, Reproduce... that can't be right—she felt Wayne lean away from her to speak to the stranger on his right, and she felt the same mix of panic and relief she had been feeling for the two weeks since the diagnosis. Driving away from the house to go to work, for the first two blocks or so, she felt an elastic band that stretched from her breastbone to Wayne, stretched until it almost sang out from tension, then the blissful snap as she pictured the parking lot, the lobby, the front desk, the secretary, her cubicle, where she had changed her password from "Waynesgirl" to "Damnitall" and turned her picture of Wayne at an angle so she would not catch sight of his face unexpectedly and start crying. At home, she had shifted the vase they bought in Tampico to a spot in front of their wedding picture and the silver anniversary portrait the girls had insisted on. Wayne had been a strong, hopeful groom, but twenty-five years later, his body seemed to tilt to one side, as though he were leaning away from Cheryl, whose face in both pictures had the dazed look she always had in pictures, trying not to blink.

Wayne and his neighbor, whose nametag said "Bill," continued to talk under the noise of the speaker's voice, and Cheryl didn't want to have to know what they said. She listened again to the doctor, a warm, olive-skinned man, so young that he could probably view his wedding pictures with neither nostalgia nor regret. He seemed miraculously untouched by the palpable pain, insulated by his PowerPoint from having to speak the hard truth, by the bright lights from having to register the dim misery in the room.

She wanted, suddenly, to breach the membrane that separated the viable from the failing—she wanted to hit the doctor, slap him across his casually healthy young professional face. She wanted to yell at him to quit talking and fix it, to bring him back.

"It's a balancing act, " he said. The PowerPoint slide said "Balancing Act" and displayed a clip-art juggler. She looked down at her notes: Anticholinergic drugs

217

reduce tremor, but cause hallucinations and confusion. Beta-blockers improve movement, but cause fainting and possible falls. Pergolide treats the depression caused by dopamine agonists, but may increase tremor.

It's not a balancing act," Cheryl thought. "It's a train wreck." She pictured four clip-art locomotives speeding toward a collision at the center of the slide.

Wayne's left hand lay on the table on the seminar packet, next to the Azilect ballpoint pen and Mirapex notepad thoughtfully provided for each participant. His hand, the hand that had loved her and worked for her, now looked inert and waxy, uninhabited and spiritless with a slight tremor running through it like the hum of a self-defrosting refrigerator.

Cheryl wished she hadn't told anyone because it didn't seem to help. Her sister-in-law had said that now she would have to be strong, strong for both of them. It was a bewildering thing to say. Cheryl wondered if she should join a gym and work out so that she could shore up, or push, or lift, or keep Wayne from attacking her. The doctor had started talking about dementia, hallucinations, and hypersexuality.

"I should lose weight," she thought. "I should lose 35, no 40 pounds." She was suddenly aware of all the candy in the room, in baskets or scattered on the vendor tables positioned around the periphery. A non-profit to install safety bars and ramps in the home offered tiny chocolate bars. A respite program for caregivers was pushing little packets of M&Ms—there's respite for you. A care home displayed gooey pastries in white frilled paper cups that looked too messy even for Cheryl.

Behind her she could hear the bright heel taps of several young women who were there to help with the event, as they moved around the room picking up slips of paper with participants' questions on them. The doctor was reading the questions aloud, and then trying to answer them, though the gist of the answers seemed to be "It varies" and "Nothing really works." Cheryl picked up her Azilect pen and a slip of Mirapex paper. "What is the best way to commit suicide?" she wrote, but then she wadded the paper up and dropped it on the floor.

Finally, a round of applause for the speaker, and the audience began to collect themselves, their jackets, their packets and Azilect pens. It was the same sad parade going out as it had been coming in, between a display of busts of past Masonic officials, their faces embarrassingly realistic depictions of various character defects—pride, avarice, lust. The halt, the lame, and the caregivers exited between them in a jerky procession.

Eyes met and slid away, not because two strangers had happened to look at each other at the same time, but because there was nothing anyone could do. To smile pleasantly, it seemed to Cheryl, would be an insult under the circumstances, like stopping to pass the time of day with a man ascending the gallows.

Cheryl and Wayne walked wordlessly out to the parking lot, her left hand in his strong right. When the car doors had crunched shut, they turned in their seats and looked at each other.

"How was that?" Wayne asked. He seemed to Cheryl at that moment like a stranger, a complete unknown, an imposter, a carjacker. His face was already showing traces of the Parkinson's mask, slackness around the jaw, expressionless eyes, Wayne's soft brown eyes that she loved, that were supposed to love her.

"Well, I don't have the screaming meemies yet," she said. "How about you?"

"I guess we'll get used to it," he said. "At least we'll have plenty of time to get used to it. It sounds like years, probably."

Cheryl turned her face away. Years was a long time.

"Don't cry," Wayne said. "I'm not dead yet. Don't cry, Sweetheart."

"I'm not crying," Cheryl said. "I'm thinking what to do."

As Wayne drove carefully home, Cheryl thought about telling the girls and dreaded it. They still depended on Wayne for so much. They had both been Daddy's girls, right from the start, like Cheryl. She still missed her own daddy, now ten years dead. She tried to remember Daddy's face, and it swam into her inner view, a round, full face with a look of confidence seemingly built into the features, the look that had made him such a good salesman, even better than Wayne, Cheryl thought.

She suddenly remembered the day when he had volunteered to take the family calico, Pansy, to the vet for a bothersome lump on her front leg. It must have been one of the few weekends when he was home instead of out in the field. She had helped him corner Pansy and then push her, protesting, into the carrier.

Mother had said, "It's probably just a foxtail. I try to check her feet every day, but you know how she is."

At seven, Cheryl had just graduated from little kid scissors, so she was sitting on the floor cutting out Care Bear paper dolls with the sharp, black-handled scissors from the utility drawer when Daddy got home from the vet, swinging into the room with the cat carrier and announcing, "The vet said it might be cancer, so I just had her put to sleep."

Cheryl remembered the shock on her mother's face as she sprang from the couch, her mouth drawn into a silent no, her hands held out in front of her as though she expected him to hand her something. Daddy said, "I figure it's better than going through all that expense and trouble. And just look at this little fellow I brought home!"

Cheryl remembered the fuzzy gray kitten stepping cautiously from the cat carrier, though she couldn't remember what had ever become of it. And she couldn't remember how she had felt at all.

"Don't worry," Wayne said, breaking the silence. "It sounds like I could last for years. We have plenty of time to plan."

It seemed to Cheryl for the first time that the future did not belong to her at all, that the future belonged only to Wayne, Wayne the stranger who was breaking her heart. It seemed to her that three tracks stretched out in front of her. Of course, there was the busy commercial street they were driving down, with shops and gas stations and restaurants that should have been familiar and comforting, places belonging to the present that had been torn away from her and turned into an incongruous past. There was also the wide silver road she had expected to ride into the future, smoothed out by Wayne's careful attention to details and enlivened with retirement, travel, family parties, and grandchild stay-overs. She could still envision it, but it was no longer within her reach. The third road, the bitter one revealed today, the one to which she seemed to be condemned, was little more than a muddy path straggling up the side of a sodden hill, the flow of brown water increasing, the ravine flooding, more mud, more rocks, a landslide, the threat of losing her footing and being dragged under, and always this burden now entrusted to her, encumbering her steps, throwing her off balance, and no way to put him down. But this was Wayne, her one, the love of her life, and that made all the difference.

The future had always been unknown whether she let herself know it or not. In the crucible of time, all these roads now before her would run together and be transformed from visions to experience to memories. She and Wayne would hold on as long as was given. She would carry him when he failed, and the end would arrive in its own mysterious way.

The Iris in the Garden

(an excerpt from a novel)

Deborah remembered very little about her parents. Such great care was taken to shield her from a grief too heavy for a young child to bear that it had taken her several days to realize that her parents had died and were not coming back. She knew they were gone; she had been told they were going to New York, and then everyone had been crying and trying to be brave. She was not surprised that Grandma Gussie was sad that they were gone; Grandma Gussie loved them all. That's why she had come to stay while they were away, to take care of Deborah. She herself wept a little when their carriage had pulled away. But it was surprising that the servants, even her nurse Katie, would miss them so much.

In the morning of the day they left, her father looking as clean and trim as a nutcracker, her mother flustered like a peony in the wind, there had been bustling and last-minute reminders to lock up the gates, to watch out for the wobbly club chair in the foyer, frantic searches to find misplaced luggage, a reminder to Grandma Gussie to call Dr. Foster if Deborah's cough returned, last hugs, just one more thing, hugs again, and they were off. The house had seemed very quiet then, and darker; Deborah wished she had been taken in the carriage to catch the train to New York to see the new statue, larger than the tallest building in St. Louis, instead of being left at home to be minded by Grandma Gussie.

After lunch, there had been messengers, shocked voices, worried looks, and Katie took her to the park for a second time that day, even though it was time for her rest and she had already fed the ducks and skipped around the pond once in each direction. As a result, she was petulant, pulling at Katie's arm, teasing her to go home, expecting sharp words and the hot little sparks that flew out of Katie's eyes when she was annoyed, but Katie was gentle and patient with her and bought her a little wind-up duck from a sidewalk vendor to occupy her, which was a delightful novelty until it foundered and sank sideways into the water, too far out of reach to retrieve.

That night as she had supper with Katie in the nursery, she again heard hushed voices and doors closing, but Katie started telling fairy stories to distract her, stories about princesses and enchantments and magical stones and talking birds, stories that were usually rationed out one at a time when Katie was in a good mood or Deborah was sick. She heard her parents' door close and expected, for just a moment, that her mother would come in for a nighttime kiss, but her parents, she remembered, were gone. Instead, Dr. Foster had come in to see her, talking to her in a soft, jolly voice. She could feel him exchanging looks with Katie over her head, more than grown-ups usually did. Deborah set aside her curiosity until later, when Katie would tuck her in and disappear up the narrow stairs to her own narrow bed, taking the candle and leaving Deborah with only moonlight to mark her way. But a lamp had been left burning in the hallway outside her parents' bedroom, the heart of the mysterious flurry. Had they come back?

Ordinarily, she was barred from her parents' room, though she was sometimes allowed to enter on Christmas and birthday mornings, spreading out the gifts and treats on the eiderdown and nestling into the warm space between them, reveling in her mother's flowery smell, petting her father's scratchy face and her mother's soft one, snuggling close. She thought now that she would just open their door a crack and see if they had returned. She would be quiet as a mouse. As she carefully pushed the door open, the beam of light from the hall lit up her mother, lying very still, alone in the middle of the big bed. Deborah started to cross over to see her. The light seemed to shine out of her mother's white face, but then the light went out, and Deborah felt her way back through the dark room, cracking her face against the doorframe, and that was why she cried once she had regained her own bed.

"My poor dear child," Grandma Gussie said in the morning. Her face looked more creased than yesterday, like a toy bear that had lost some of its stuffing. "Your parents, your father and your mother…your parents…I'm so sorry, my darling." Her voice cracked, and she shook herself to try again. "They're gone. But I will be here to look after you."

"I know," Deborah said. That arrangement had already been explained to her. "They've gone to New York to see the new statue."

Grandma Gussie turned away, and Deborah could tell she was crying by the way her shoulders moved. She walked away with her hands to her face, bent forward as though making her way through a strong wind, and called for Katie, who came in and sat on the low chair by the fireplace, taking Deborah onto her lap even though she had said the last time that Deborah was grown too big and heavy to cosset. Her own little sisters, she had said, were doing the washing up to help their mother by the time they were her age.

"Your parents are not in New York, Deborah.

They've gone to heaven to be with God."

"Why? Why not New York?"

Katie set her face, the way she did when she wanted to do one thing and had to do another instead. "There was a terrible carriage accident on the way to the train station. They died, my dear. Your father was gone, was dead in the instant. Your dear mother was so badly hurt—there was nothing the doctors could do for her. She died in the night. Do you understand now? That's why Doctor Foster was here."

"When are they coming back?"

"They won't be coming back to this world, that's certain. But if you're a good girl and lead a good life, then you will join them in heaven."

"When?"

"When you are a very old lady with white hair and grandchildren of your own and the good Lord calls you away. Until then, you've just to say your prayers and be a good girl."

Deborah wriggled off of Katie's lap and looked out the nursery window into the garden. It seemed farther away than it had the day before. She wondered if she had grown taller to make it seem so small. The sunlight streamed out of the throats of the irises below, where it seemed for the moment as though the light had blurred, diffused, and disappeared when the clouds thickened and the air outside cooled the window against Deborah's hot forehead. She felt, in the dark space inside her chest, that when the light came back, it would be darker, tinged with the flavor of tears. Mornings would come again, but she was alone in a new way, and the next morning would follow and the next until all the light was gone.

The next year, Deborah tried to paint the irises in the garden, the fuzzy purple, speckled brown petals and the fierce onslaught of gold that came from their throats. Ever since she could remember, she had made pictures, working in secret under the nursery table, shielded by the drooping tablecloth, drawing mostly horses and princesses, the hair on both curling into fantastical shapes, their expressions haughty and grand, but the garden began to attract her attention as spring came and the iris bloomed bravely among the bobbing peonies. With Grandma Gussie's permission, she took her paint box and easel down with her before lunchtime and drew from life for the first time. It was an enchanting experience. The path from her eye to her hand seemed to pass through her singing heart. The picture on the paper wasn't right, it wasn't quite what she saw, but the next one was better as she planned where to place the stems, how to put one blossom in front of another. When her best picture was finished, she took it shyly to give Grandma Gussie, who was fond of flowers and had many a still life on the walls of her room, though these were dark pictures, the only bright spots the shine of a distant window on the curve of a teapot or the eye of a dead pheasant laid across the fruit.

"Oh my, very strong," Grandma Gussie had said. "Very strong and very…warm." Her kind face had looked concerned as she studied the purple petals, which faded onto the page, and the golden hearts of the flowers, the center from which the light seemed to stream most insistently. "Very strong, indeed." Her voice sounded troubled, as though alarmed at the revelation that the light shining for Deborah was too warm, too strong, the flowers invested with a bold physicality that surely was not intentional.

"Shall I make one for Tante Charity?" Deborah dreaded Tante Charity's yearly visits, but such a gift of living light would surely please anyone, especially someone whose stony gray eyes seemed to see only what needed to be corrected. Nothing about the irises needed to be fixed.

"I'll put this away with my treasures," Grandma Gussie said. "It's too fine to put up where it could get ruined." She carefully laid the picture in the crease of her book and closed it cautiously. "And how would you like to have a drawing master? Someone to show you how to draw whatever you like?"

The picture Grandma Gussie didn't see, the one that would have troubled her much more, was Deborah's picture of Katie's arm. Katie had been leaning on the windowsill, her sleeves rolled up high, revealing her round, rosy, speckled arm, pink dimpled skin on the side that met the sun, a creamy white on its inner curve. She was looking out to see if the apothecary's boy was coming along the street. If he was, she would turn her head away and ignore him, even if he whistled at her. Impudent scamp. She was surprised when she glanced down to see Deborah sitting on the floor, her pastels next to her, drawing tablet on her lap, looking at her and changing the color of her chalk rapidly, her tongue caught between her teeth.

"Good heavens! You've made me all fat and speckledy! How could you be so naughty? You're a wicked child, you are!"

"You are speckledy, Katie. That's what your arm is like to me." And Deborah threw herself at Katie, wrapping her arms tightly around the speckledy, soft, vital arm that she loved to watch lifting the kettle from the hob, wringing out the washcloth to wash her face after supper, the muscles bunching under the speckledy skin and the soft layer under it, the arm she loved to look at and to draw. "I love your arm." And she kissed Katie's arm over and over to show it was so.

"Please, Miss Deborah, leave off. You're like a crazy whelp, you are. Leave off! What would your grandma say to see you acting so?"

Deborah left off, but kept the picture in her folder. And to make up with Katie, who seemed affronted, she drew a painstaking picture of Katie's new hat, a gorgeous black straw creation trimmed with grosgrain ribbon in an elegant bow, chiffon draping, shiny black berries, a curling white feather, and a knot of cunningly crafted white silk roses. This, unfortunately, was the picture she showed Tante Charity on her next visit, thinking that since Tante Charity wore an elaborate hat every time she left the house, whether for church, shopping, or visiting, she would surely appreciate the beauty of this beautiful portrait of Katie's beautiful hat.

"It's a picture of Katie's hat, Tante Charity. I made it for you."

"Indeed!" was all Tante Charity had said, studying Deborah's work and then turning her punishing eye as if to seek out the offending headpiece. "Augusta!" she ordered, as she always did, and Grandma Gussie hurried to answer her, following the pattern of a long lifetime of obedience to the iron will of her older sister.

"Of course, Charity. Whatever is the matter?"

"We must speak of this...hat." Tante Charity turned her eye to Deborah, and then swept Grandma Gussie out into the hall and down the stairs for a private conference, the offending picture held between fastidious finger and thumb. Deborah didn't know what she had done, but she knew it must have been wrong. There was no pleasing Tante Charity unless one presented her with a face as cold and placid and unchanging as a painted china plate. That was the face she was trying to learn. It was the face, she often thought, that all the grown-up women wore.

That night, she saw Katie taking her hat off of the bureau and wrapping it in tissue to store in its box. She slid the box under the bureau and turned away. Her eyes were red, and her lips twisted as though to hold back hot words.

"Won't you want to wear it to Mass tomorrow?" Deborah had asked.

"No, miss, I won't. Evidently it's too good for the likes of me." Katie left the room without her usual kind goodnight, and Deborah puzzled about it as she went to sleep.

The sorrow of losing her mother and father still colored her dreams, dreams in which a carriage lay on its side, one wheel still spinning, dreams of darkness creeping down the hall like a fog, of a heartless woman as tall as a building crushing her way through St. Louis, sowing tears. She had imagined in her waking hours clinging to the two of them, not letting them get into the carriage, insisting on going with them, but she didn't know there would be an accident. No one knew. She had cried and grieved for that early loss until it was part of her, like a secret organ tucked inside her body, ticking away.

But now she had done something, had caused something bad to happen to Katie, and it was different than an accident. She realized now for the first time how dangerous even a peaceful life, a small gesture, an impulse could be, how dangerous to love something and let it show.

Grandma Gussie, although bewildered by her granddaughter's way of painting, was as good as her word. For Deborah's ninth birthday, she was to have art lessons, though not from a drawing master. It was felt she was too young to bear up under the exacting scrutiny and serious demands of a male tutor, whose focus would necessarily be on ambitious works of art, on the techniques of greatness. It would be too strenuous for a little girl who only painted flowers. Instead a suitable, gentler, less expensive alternative would be found among the many female art students who served the muse, espousing a softer, more diffuse approach with room for even a nine-year-old's talents to bloom. So every Tuesday and Friday, when Deborah ran home from St. Agnes Girls' School, she dashed up the stairs to set up her easel, palette, and paints to be ready for the arrival of Miss Jean Singleton, her art teacher.

At first, Deborah had been afraid of her stiff back, her expressionless face and the suffering in her eyes. She didn't want to learn suffering. She wanted to learn how to be truer to her vision of the world, to bring her hands and eyes into a vibrant harmony. She wanted to learn how to do real horses, horses running, horses as real as flowers, and real faces, real hair. And dreams. But once she showed Miss Singleton some of her pictures—another one of irises, Katie's arm, a second, sadder version of Katie's hat, a particularly nice pretend horse—Miss Singleton seemed to soften and looked at her kindly, with a gleam of sympathy.

"These are very good, Deborah. This lets me know where to start." Miss Singleton set up a pomegranate, a blue vase with white flowers drooping down its sides, and a pair of Deborah's white gloves draped together in the foreground.

"What do you see, Deborah? First, we must use our eyes. Then, and only then, are we ready to draw."

Deborah stared at the still life. She squinted. She turned her head to one side and then the other.

"I see finger marks on the vase. I see the rough part on the glove where I chew on it when I'm bored during Mass. And blue streaks in the pomegranate, like the veins in my arm. The flowers look desperate. Did you put water in the vase for them?"

Miss Singleton rose silently and carried the water ewer from beside Deborah's bed over to the vase, where she carefully poured.

"Now?"

"In a while," Deborah said. "They're just starting to drink."

They sat together quietly, looking at the little tableau. Then Deborah, looking sideways at Miss Singleton for her permission, picked up her special art pencil and started to draw.

This was their first lesson, but it set the tone for their times together. They were contented in each other's company, but never merry, sharing nothing but the look of things and the way outlines could communicate shape, and perspective could communicate distance, and small colors could blend into glorious large spaces. At first Deborah was compliant, but as the lessons became more familiar, as she came to know Miss Singleton, the breadth but also the limits of her vision, the student began to push against those limits. Sometimes they argued.

"You're not painting what you see today, Deborah. Use your eyes, not your imagination."

"You want me to paint what everyone else sees, so that they can be nice and say, 'Oh what a lovely tree!'

I just painted what I see. It's growing and waiting. It's hard, not lovely at all, but strong and bitter, like that," she said, pointing at the bleak tree on her page, a tree that soaked up light and held it.

"You paint it both ways, then," Miss Singleton suggested. "One for everyone else, and one just for yourself." They drew together in amicable silence then, many versions of this little sapling in the garden, a pear tree which was too young to bear fruit but still inspired them to draw it in their various ways, standing resolute, vulnerable, untried, doomed, a study in line, tender colors or bold, an interruption of the ground and sky, a slash, a springing line, a pear tree in all seasons.

The pictures Deborah painted in secret, just for herself, were not the still life arrangements or garden scenes of her lessons, but private images pulled out of her dreams, lurid, indistinct, twisted figures that rose up out of oceans of color: flying trees, a red wheel spinning through the sky, the faces of witches, the stars on fire. Miss Singleton would never be called on to appraise and correct these unorthodox pieces. Grandma Gussie would never be distressed by the hot, gyrating world of Deborah's untutored imagination

Because of Deborah's progress as a student, Miss Singleton received permission to take her to see the Corot exhibit at Forest Park, skipping a whole day of school in order to ride the streetcar to the museum and see the paintings without the interference and noise of the inevitable weekend crowd. They stood at each painting like true votaries, exploring, probing, discovering, accepting, and sometimes floating away into the cool atmosphere of a lake scene, a willow, a bridge. Then a few short steps to the next station and the next haunting landscape.

"This one is too proud," Deborah said. "It's not coming through the same eyes. It's not as real as the others."

"Perhaps not," Miss Singleton said. "I rather like it though."

After the long morning of looking, Deborah's eyes were tired and full of images. They stopped at the teashop for a quick tea and a sugar bun for lunch.

"Can you see what a great master he is? A genius, a truly great painter! It's such a fine opportunity for you to see paintings from famous collections. What did you learn from Corot today, Deborah?"

"He paints light like it's water," she said. "And water like it's mud." Deborah saw from Miss Singleton's face that she had said the wrong thing. "Shiny mud," she amended, hoping to make it right.

Miss Singleton laughed, the first time Deborah had seen her face lose its caution long enough to brighten, and she set her cup down in the saucer. "Let's walk down to the lagoon, shall we? We can look at some water that is water."

That night as a tired, satisfied Deborah laid her head on her pillow, the paintings were still there, dancing and tumbling in gentle colors behind her closed eyes. And she hoped as she fell asleep that she would live to be an old lady, as Katie had almost promised, so she would have time to paint everything in the world, everything she could imagine, everything that mattered. And in time, when she was grown up and could go wherever she wanted, she would go and paint the monstrous face of the statue that had stolen her mother and father, the cold indifferent stone woman set on an island in New York to lure people to their deaths.

Acknowledgements

I want to thank my teachers at CSU Chico: Clark Brown, Gary Thompson, Carole Oles, Thia Wolf, and Lois Bueler. Thanks also to Zoe Keithley of the Sacramento Story Workshop, and Meg Files of the Pima Writers Workshop. In addition I am grateful to Dean of English Tammy Montgomery and the SummerWords faculty and administration at American River College for their support of this project and writing in general. Thanks to Karen Burchett and Michael Angelone for their work on the Ad Lumen editorial board and to Don Reid for typesetting this slender volume. My perpetual appreciation goes to Christian Kiefer, my editor at Ad Lumen Press and boon companion in the pursuit of literary adventure.

Thanks to Melinda Lightfoot for her editorial, readerly, and sisterly input, to Coda Hale for making my life interesting, and to Jim Abraham for bringing the phrase "body of work" to my attention.

My deepest gratitude belongs to Adair Landborn, who has been listening to my stories with an open heart from the very beginning and whose feedback and understanding have always inspired me to do my best.

About the Author

Lois Ann Abraham is a professor of English at American River College and a prize-winning fiction writer. Her pieces have appeared in *Sojourner, Chico News & Review, Writing on the Edge, inside english, Burning the Little Candle,* and *Convergences.* She spent her formative years in Texas, the Panhandle of Oklahoma, and New Mexico, where she still has strong roots. She presently lives in a Sacramento house with no ninety-degree angles, along with her husband and her calico cat, Ella Fitzgerald.